DARK POWER

DARK POWER

DARKHAVEN SAGA: BOOK EIGHT

DANIELLE ROSE

WATERHOUSE PRESS

For Martha

ONE

The concept of time is fascinating.

After Will and Amicia died, my nestmates were broken, left to pick up the shattered pieces of our lives while the world forgot about our fallen comrades. Time did what it always does—moves on, the seconds ticking by in steady streams like blood pulsing through my heart.

Losing them nearly destroyed me. Until one day, it didn't. I was fine. I just had to *stop* thinking about them.

Until now.

Because now, death is all I can think about. Death and time.

I think about my mother, about all the things she told me about the undead—some true, some not. I tell myself the rogue vampire staring back at me is not my father, yet he wears his face like a wickedly cruel and obnoxiously deceitful mask.

There are lines etched in the corners of his eyes and silver in his hair. His usually tan skin is paler now. He is still tall and lean, and as he smiles at me, showcasing two pointed fangs, his cheeks dimple. He looks exactly like I remember—except for all the features that make him a vampire.

His irises are crimson, and the soul that should swirl like magic within them looks dead.

Mamá warned me that this day might come, that true evil

1

would reveal itself to me in the shape of someone I love. It will be formidable, but my resolve must be more resilient. I cannot falter. I cannot succumb to its will.

"*Debes ser fuerte, hija,*" my mother would say, reminding me that I must remain strong when I am faced with my harshest reality.

El Diablo intenta engañarte . . .

Her words echo in my mind, her warning of trickery as raw and real as the red-hot flesh sizzling in my palm.

Only moments ago, the black onyx crystal denied my request for aid, choosing instead to strike me down. Its lashing mirrored its attack from earlier tonight, when I was lost in the forest and desperate enough to harness its magic to locate this rogue nest.

My mother taught me vampires are evil creatures, but what she really meant to say is *rogue vampires*. It is *rogue* vampires that the hunters have warned me about. These soulless abominations are ruled by their hunger, by the blood lust. They do not value life, and they certainly have no desire to coexist.

But if this is true, if rogue vampires are as evil as I have come to believe, why am I still breathing? Why am I not fighting for my life in what is so obviously an outnumbered and lopsided battle?

"*Te he echado de menos, hija,*" Papá says.

When he smiles at me, the lines in his skin deepen. It is a stark contrast to the face I see when he does not smile. When he is neutral, his skin is smoother, making him appear younger. But when it creases, the mask is revealed, and it is so startling, I want to reach forward and rip it off. This is the face I look at right now, the one that reminds me this vampire can't possibly be my father.

"I have missed you too," I say, responding to his earlier sentiment.

I speak the truth, but I do not yearn for an impostor. Still, the honesty of my words cut straight through to my heart. They plunge deep, like worms burrowing through the softened earth, and tears threaten, stinging my eyes where they pool at the corners. I refuse to release them. I can't show weakness, even if I am one soft breeze away from crumbling.

The cave system the rogues have made into their home is vast and dense, a labyrinth of interconnected tunnels that lead deeper into the abyss. Even though I have explored much of this space while searching for the rogue nest, I know I have seen only a small fraction of it. And that thought terrifies me. What else will I encounter? How many more rogue vampires are surrounding me?

As I stand with my father in a small passageway, I am acutely aware of what is in the room behind me. My skin prickles, my senses alerting me to the dozens, if not hundreds, of rogue vampires watching me, waiting for the directive to end my life.

I was taught control is impossible. The hunters said rogue vampires are incapable of leadership, but clearly, that is not true. Amicia's assurances, the hunters' promises, the witches' lies . . . Too much of what I have learned is not true.

What if the hunters' intentions are no different than the witches' intentions? What if they are using my abilities to further their personal agenda: to wipe out a superior race? Rogues, by nature, are stronger and faster, but clearly, they are also capable of self-control. If they weren't, they would be attacking. And I would be dead.

My thoughts may be racing—hopefully making me worry for nothing—but one thing is certain: The vampires lied. The witches lied too.

Can I trust anyone anymore?

"*Hija?*" my father says, garnering my attention. "*¿Estás bien?*"

I nod, but uneasiness continues to rise in my chest, like bubbling bile burning the back of my throat. Every fiber of my body wants to flee, to run from the caves and escape the rogue army at my back.

But I can't leave. It's daylight, and even though I know the sun will kill me, the words spill from my lips.

"I want to leave," I say firmly.

Again, my father smiles at me, eyes sparkling with admiration. I have seen this very look countless times. He always appreciated my headstrong, stubborn personality—much more than Mamá ever did. She wanted to extinguish this quality, turning me into a drone who survives on following orders, while Papá wanted to nurture it. He knew I was destined to lead our coven, and a good leader is no drone.

The lines etched around his eyes are sunken crevices now. Wrinkles alone are a jolting sight. Most of the vampires I encounter were turned at a young age, forever marked in history as a teen or young adult. But my father was older when he died, and the remnants of his age punctuate everything he does, from the way he looks to the way he sounds to the way he moves.

When I look at him, even though I know I shouldn't, I can see past his piercing crimson irises and pale skin. I can block out all the things that make him a vampire and see only what made him mortal—his salt-and-pepper hair, his age, the scars

4

from previous battles. I see the man who cradled me in his arms, not the monster who stole his mortality.

I want so desperately to believe he is the same person who helped birth me, who gave me his life's blood to bring me into this world.

"You can't leave, *hija*," he says, accent thick like the stagnant air.

The smell of rotting flesh wafts closer, reaching my nostrils, and I gag, choking on the scent. If he notices my reaction, he does not mention it.

I want to beg for my release, and I even succeed in convincing myself he might actually let me go. Because he wears the skin of my father, and Papá was a good man. He would grant me this one request.

"¡Por favor!" I screech, the sound deafening in this small space.

"*El sol está brillando*," he says quietly. He points at the sky with his finger, but I don't look up. We are deep within the cave, surrounded by slick, grimy walls. I see no sky, no sun. There are no stars, no moon to offer me strength.

Papá might have just reminded me that the sun is shining, but it's what he *doesn't* say that leaves me chilled. Because whether I like it or not, I am trapped. I can't leave until sunset, but by then, I fear I may not be alive to greet the night.

"You are safe here, daughter," he says, answering my thoughts.

I want to believe him. I want to trust that his word is as unbreakable as his promises once were.

I crane my neck, peering over my shoulder, and attempt to turn and look at the rogues scattered behind me. But I don't want to take my eyes off the vampire in front of me either. Of course, this doesn't work. I cannot look in two directions at the same time, so I end up looking at neither.

My gaze washes over the jagged stone walls that are dripping with filth, and I squirm internally. The muck has pooled at my feet, and my boots make a squishing sound as I teeter from foot to foot. Unfortunately, the sound from my movement isn't capable of distracting the vampires from hearing my overworked heart. It beats incessantly in my head, so loud I almost don't hear my father speak.

"Consider this an opportunity," he says.

"To die?" I counter.

"To learn," he clarifies. "You can't leave until the sun sets, and we have only just been reunited."

TWO

I miss darkness—the *true* darkness. The very one that resides within the crystal hanging from my neck. I miss its certainty, because even though it haunted me, I knew the evil that lurked within the stone. I knew what to expect even though I failed to protect myself against it. This place, with its cavern of trickster tunnels—ones that end abruptly and others with hidden entrances—is a new darkness. A fresh hell crafted just for me.

For us.

This prison is dank and moldy and crowded, and I don't know what to expect or how to protect myself. I have no friends here, no one to help count the hours until daylight. No one to assure me that I will survive to see nightfall.

I am alone.

Even my darkness is mute, paving the way for the echoing, vicious screams of my heart to radiate within the confines of my mind. My anguish is loud, muffled only when my father speaks.

"*Camina conmigo, niña*," he says.

Papá asks me to walk with him, but my legs are rooted in place. I may not be moving physically, but I can still feel myself burrowing deep, searching for another means of escape. Because if I cannot walk to freedom, then I shall dig and crawl and tunnel my way home. But is there a *home* to go back to?

I stare at him, still unresponsive. Papá looks different than the others. It is easy to spot a rogue vampire. They are as distinguishable as raw meat and seared flesh. They smell rotten, and although I am sure it isn't possible, their skin looks so pale it is almost translucent. It is pure white with the slightest hint of pale blue, like the new-fallen snow. That sheer crystal color makes their eyes breathtaking in all the worst ways. Their crimson irises are an unmoving, blood-red color, deeper in tone than the bright crimson hue I am used to seeing.

Every rogue vampire in this cave fits this description except for one. Except for *him*.

"Come, daughter," he says, repeating himself.

This time, I obey, legs heavy. I drag my heels, boots skidding against the rocky ground as I move closer until we share the same breath space. The odor wafting from him makes me scrunch my nose, but it doesn't compare to the scent coming from behind me. Only a few feet away, dozens and dozens of rogue vampires stand tall, their stench making the acrid taste in my mouth a pleasantry. Bile creeps up my esophagus, spilling into my mouth, and it tastes like stale blood. I swallow it down.

When I stand at his side, he reaches for me, and I freeze, breath caught in my throat, spine tingling from fear, limbs shaking. Everything happens all at once, and it takes every ounce of courage I have left to keep my knees from buckling. I want to scream, to dash away, to put so much distance between us even my heightened senses will fail. But I don't.

He tucks a loose strand of hair behind my ear, fingertips grazing my cheek. My blood runs cold, body icy where his skin touches mine. This overwhelming sense of dread is familiar. I feel this way anytime I am near a rogue, and the realization affirms my original thought: this monster can't possibly be my father.

But then he speaks, and his accent is just how I remember it. He smiles at me, the mask becoming more recognizable as he ages before my eyes, wrinkles deepening in prominence. And I try not to see the monster. I want to see the man.

"Let us walk," he says. "We have much to discuss."

The rogues stay behind as I follow him through the tunnel, allowing me the private time I so desperately desire. I have so many questions for him about that day, about what happened when Mamá carried me away in her arms, leaving him behind. She told me once that she went back one day and found his remains, burning them to be certain he would not wake to an eternal life of blood and death.

Obviously, that was a lie. One small deception in a sea of dishonesty.

Each step that grants distance between the army and me allows my head to clear, the weight of it falling off my chest like a heavy blanket. I catch myself peering up at him, staring at his thick, bushy brows and his sharp, angular nose. His hair is longer than I remember it to be. It falls loosely, covering his ears but not reaching his jawline. His Adam's apple is prominent and bobs as he swallows.

I wonder what he is thinking about, if he knows I am watching him, if he plans to spill his secrets about the decade he has spent as a vampire. I consider telling him about my transition, about my ability to access magic, but my lips are numb to the truth. Until I understand his intentions, the real reason he returned to Darkhaven, I can't reveal my deepest secret.

The path he has chosen leads us to a larger room that

offers even more channels, and soon, we are deep within the cave system, far from anything that looks familiar. I know I am in danger, yet I cannot stop myself from plunging into the unknown.

As we walk, we dodge streams of lights that cascade down, and I find myself meeting his stride, as though it hasn't been years since we last saw each other. He keeps his gaze focused ahead, never glancing over at me. But I still watch him, imprinting his features in my mind.

"*Tienes preguntas para mi,*" he says finally. He speaks simply, matter of factly, as though he already knows my inner turmoil.

"Yes, I have questions."

"¿Que quieres saber?" he asks.

I huff, a burst of air expelled from my chest so forcefully it erupts around us, the exasperated sound bouncing off the slick walls. Immediately, I am embarrassed. Seeing my father so soon after losing my mother has left me more emotional than I care to admit.

"I want to know everything," I say. "Tell me about that day, about that time in the forest when—"

"When your mother left me?" he interrupts.

I swallow hard and nod. "I want to know about your life."

"I should have died a mortal death that day," he says.

"But you were reborn."

"*Como tú,*" he says.

"Like me," I whisper, repeating his words.

I think a lot about the day I transitioned, that night I asked Jasik to save my life so I could help my coven. I didn't know much about vampirism then. I certainly didn't know I would fall unconscious and wake several hours later. Had

I known that, I wonder if I would have asked him to save me or if I would have asked him to save *them*. I think I would have. I would have made him walk away, leaving me to bleed out while he saved my coven. It's funny how far loyalty takes a person. I would have sunk my athame into my heart if that meant protecting my family. I am glad I didn't.

"*Cuéntame de tú muerte*," he says.

"I died the night of a full moon ritual," I begin, prepared to rehash the details of my death. "Rogue vampires attacked, and I was without my stake."

"Rogue vampires?" he asks, brow furrowed.

I nod. "Rogue... Like you."

He chuckles. "Do I appear rogue to you?"

I take my time to respond, letting the question linger between us, because the truth is, no, he doesn't.

I kick at the ground, sending a shower of gunk splattering before us. The peek holes in the stone allow the light and moisture to spew down, but once inside, it has nowhere to go. The air is thick and damp, coating my lungs in sludge. I hack, still unprepared to answer his question.

"There are no rogue vampires," he says finally. "There are only vampires, *hija*. Mortals and immortals. That is all."

"I was taught rogue vampires aren't like the rest of us," I explain.

"¿Quién te enseñó esto?" he asks.

I refrain from mentioning the other hunters and instead place blame on someone who can't defend herself.

"Mamá," I say, immediately ashamed. "She taught me this."

Mamá was a lot of things—for instance, she was a spectacularly terrible mother—but she really did believe all vampires were evil. I don't consider that admission from her to be a lie. So mentioning her now, in this way, leaves me overwhelmed with guilt. As much as I hate Mamá for everything she did to me, I still love her.

Papá nods, returning his gaze to the path ahead.

"Do you still believe this?" he asks me.

I shrug, unable to come up with a firm answer either way. I have fought, killed, and nearly died at the hands of rogue vampires. In fact, every single rogue vampire I have encountered—except for Papá and a few of his minions—has wanted me dead. How can he expect me to believe I don't feel as though I am in danger at this very moment?

"*Lo verás*," he says. "One day, you will learn the truth. You will see that I am not lying to you."

"And what is the truth?" I ask.

He falls silent again as we exit the small passageway and spill into another large open space. There are a half dozen rogue vampires in this space, and all are feeding from a girl who is still alive. Her head is angled awkwardly, her eyes pooled with tears. She is facing me, but I don't think she sees me. Not anymore. The distant gaze is one I have seen time and time again. She is dying, on the very brink of greeting the afterlife even as I walk toward her.

Still, my instincts kick in, and my legs are already propelling me forward, thrusting me closer to save her. But I am stopped.

Papá's fingers are curled around my arm; they are long and slim but locked on tight. He will not release me. Not until I submit. I stare, shocked. He expects me to believe rogues are not monsters at the very same moment his friends are killing innocent people? He must understand my unspoken confusion, because he answers me as though I have said it aloud.

"We are *vampires*," he says. "We survive on blood."

"We don't have to kill people," I hiss.

"Have you never before?" he asks.

His accent is strong, so strong he doesn't even sound like himself. His voice is lower, deeper, *darker*. I hear the intrigue and his own disbelief. Somehow, I know that my having never taken a mortal life to sate my blood lust excites him. I also know, that when it comes to it, this is what he will ask of me. He will make me prove my allegiance to him by doing the one thing I have refused.

I yank my arm free and stumble backward, but when I turn to face the girl, she is already dead. The vacant expression on her face muffles my unspoken promise to her—the one I broke when I failed to save her.

"You have so much to learn," Papá says.

His breath is cold on the nape of my neck. It makes the loose hair flutter, the sensation prickling all the way down my spine. I face him again.

"You are a monster," I say.

"I am a vampire," he clarifies. "We are not monsters, though we are born from the darkness."

I panic at his words and move to clutch the amulet at my chest. Something stops me, halts me as my arm snaps upward, hand never reaching the stone. It's his eyes. They have moved from mine to the amulet. And all at once, I am sure.

He knows.

He knows what I carry, about the power that is stored within the crystal I protect. And like everyone else, he wants it for himself.

"Why did you come back?" I ask. "It has been ten years. Why now?"

I want him to say it out loud, to admit that he came for the amulet.

"*Vine por ti, hija,*" he says, with his gaze returned to mine rather than on the stone.

"For me?" I ask. "You expect me to believe that you came for me?"

"*No me crees?*" he asks.

"No," I say. "I do not believe you. If you wanted to come back for me, you would have come sooner. You wouldn't have waited until..."

"Until what?" he asks after I have trailed off.

He inches closer, his stride eager, as though I am on the verge of confession. But I am not. I remain steadfast in my decision not to tell him about the amulet, about the hunters, even about Mamá.

"Tell me why you didn't come sooner," I say firmly.

"Your mother would not have approved."

"She would not have turned you away. You were her husband."

"And you were her daughter," he says. "What did she do when you became a vampire? Did she welcome you home?"

"She was starting to believe me," I lie. "She understood that only rogue vampires are evil."

He snorts, rolling his eyes as he waves me off with his hand.

"*Tu mientes,*" he snarls.

"I am not lying!" I shout.

The words spill from my lips, the outrage dripping from my tongue a surprise even to me. I sound offended by his accusation, like I really am telling the truth. But I know I am lying. Still, my emotions have me frazzled, and it is affecting me, from memory to speech.

"Mortals cannot accept what we are because we are *better*," he says. "We are stronger, faster, smarter in every way."

His words mirror what the hunters have taught me. These very reasons are why rogue vampires are so dangerous. They are the superior vampire. Losing their soul, making that deal with the darkness, grants them more power. The strength they receive from taking lives makes them a formidable opponent.

"You only care about the blood lust," I say.

"I live for blood," Papá says, agreeing with me. "Are you telling me you do not?"

"Not the way you do," I explain. "I would never kill a human."

He smiles at me, a coy, sly grin that transforms his face from father to monster in the blink of an eye. His features are dark now, his blood-red irises morphing into something else entirely. His skin is so pale white, his eyes the color of obsidian. Even his accent is wrong. I wanted this man to be my father, but he is not. I see that now.

I stumble backward, desperate for space. I hold out my arms before me, like they alone could stop him—and the others—should he pursue me.

"Never, Ava?" he says, voice whisper soft. "Never have you ever wanted to drink from a human, to *kill* a human?"

I flash back to that moment, when I would have killed Luna had Jasik not stopped me. There have been other accidents like that in the days following my transition. I almost killed those teens and that child. If my friends hadn't stopped me, I would be a monster too.

But I didn't, and I remind myself of that. I didn't hurt those people because I have friends who love me, who have helped me transition into the protector Darkhaven deserves.

"Do you think this is the best way to convince me that you're not evil?" I counter, ignoring his question.

"I care more about you accepting what you are," he says.

And just like that, in nine short words, the monster reminds me of Jasik. My sire yearns for the very same thing—for me to accept my immortality as a gift, not a curse. Knowing I can compare the two vampires makes my heart lurch. Jasik is nothing like Papá. He is not a rogue vampire. He would never put his own self-interests above his devotion to his family, to me.

But still, there is a memory, a hint of truth, buried deep down, and as I unearth it, glimpses of my nightmare loop endlessly in my mind.

I see Jasik, and he is rogue.

THREE

Recollection is a fickle beast.

There are memories in the confines of my mind, deep within the muffled depths of my skull. Some moments I can recall with ease, summoning flashes of images like a movie reel before my eyes. Others are harder to reach. I must coax them from the darkness, piecing together my past like a jigsaw puzzle.

A few are almost completely gone. I know they are there, but no matter how hard I try to grab what is just out of reach, time has made it so they dissipate even while being dangled before me. Entire chunks of my childhood lost to the abyss, a cruel punishment for someone meant to live countless lifetimes.

The memories lost are all of my father. I remember the night he died in vivid detail, but there are other moments—less life-altering shifts in time—that are completely gone to me. And the ones that slip away are always of him.

Having just ordered the taking of a life, Papá stands a few feet away from me, asking me to follow in his footsteps—a request that leaves me unconvinced he is the same man who brought me into this world.

But he is the only being on this earth who can remind me, who can offer me clarity regarding the moments I have lost.

He may be a monster, but he is a monster with memories.

"Is this what you have been doing with the years given to you?" I ask, knowing exactly where this line of questioning will lead.

Behind him, his rogue minions have gathered, their crimson irises like glaring fireballs. They too have abandoned the girl, and I know she will remain here, forever lost to the family she left behind.

"I think you already know the answer to that, *hija*," he says.

He's right. I do. I know he has spent the last decade spreading death like a virus, taking lives as he pleases, swarming cities as a locust. He is the plague in its truest form. He wields his vampirism as a curse, morphing lost souls into his own personal army. I know he must be stopped, but it won't be by my hand. At least, not yet. Not until I get the answers I so desperately crave.

"Why do you do this?" I ask.

"Because I can," he says simply.

The truth of his words is like fire in my gut. They burn my innards, branding me with his honesty, marking my flesh as being born from his own and rooting me in this place. And somehow, I know I will remember this moment. I will forget all the others, all the times I have cherished and the faces I have loved, and I will relive these seconds as an endless loop in time. Because these are the actions I can never take back. These are the moments that define a person, and I have already made my choice.

"Tell me about that night," I say. "And about your life after."

I turn away from the dead girl who lies awkwardly on

the cold, hard ground. Her eyes are milky and white, a haze covering her once bright irises. I don't want to see their accusations anymore, so I look away, leaving her behind.

"There is nothing to tell," he says plainly.

"You died," I say. "That alone is important enough to share."

I am annoyed, growing more irritated by the second. His refusal to detail the final night we spent together makes me wonder what else he might be hiding.

"*Se que recuerdas esto,*" he says.

He believes that night is fresh in my mind, utterly unaware that I am losing my memories of him. He died when I was too young to know the importance of cherishing those moments.

"We ate lunch in the forest," he says. "And after spending too many hours in the sun, we fell asleep. We woke when it was dark, and the vampires came."

"How did they know where to find us?" I ask.

For years, I wondered how the vampires knew where we were, how they found us in the middle of a massive forest, but I was always without the courage to ask Mamá.

"We are hunters, *mi amor,*" he says, the words thick with his annoyance. "We can always find our prey."

"Mamá left you," I say. "She knew you would die."

He nods, his dark hair swaying with his assertion. "She knew."

"I'm sorry," I say.

My confession chokes from me, my breath abrupt in its wake. It bursts from my chest, lungs heaving from the anguish that coats each syllable. For years, I have held on to my guilt for being too young to help, to my regret for not stopping Mamá as she tore through the forest with me in her arms, to my terror at watching my father's slowly shrinking silhouette as the distance grew between us. Eventually, he became nothing more than a speck, my mundane senses failing me.

I apologized to him endless times over the years that have passed since that day, believing I would never be offered the chance to tell him myself.

"So am I," he says. "But not because I died."

I frown. "Then why are you sorry?"

"Because you did not die with me."

I hold my breath, tears stinging my eyes. My lungs will soon convulse, and I fancy the idea of continuing to reject their wish for oxygen. Because a quick death, that swift blanket of darkness, has to be a kinder end than what Papá has in store for me. His words alone break me, so I fear the damage his fists will cause.

"You wanted me to die," I whisper, unbelieving.

"I wanted us all to be together," he says. "If I knew then what I know now, I would have slit your throat myself. And I would have let them feed from you too."

I gasp. "You're a monster."

"No, *hija*," he says. "I already told you. I am a child of darkness. Like you."

"I am *nothing* like you," I hiss.

He *tsks* me, shaking his head.

"You are both right and wrong, *mija*," he says. "You are just like me except for one important difference."

"What?" I say, spitting the word at him.

"You are burdened by your power," he says. "I embrace what I was given, whereas you cage yourself."

"Believing in the value of human life does not mean I am caged."

"You are in denial," he says, deadpan. "You are dead, just like me, and I am not sorry that I wish we died together."

"If you wanted a family reunion so bad, why did you wait until now to come back to Darkhaven?"

"I didn't want to return," he explains. "When I woke up in the forest that night, I was alone, with nothing but my hunger. For years, I obeyed its desire for life, for souls, feeding and living and traveling the world by way of the shadows."

"It sounds like nothing has changed," I say, narrowing my gaze at him.

He chuckles and runs a hand through his tangled mane. "I see *you* have not changed. You are still as stubborn and headstrong as I remember."

"Don't change the subject," I say. "Tell me why you came back. Why now?"

"You believe there is light in this world," he says. "And you live by that hope, completely ignoring the other side. Tell me, *hija*, what has this brought you?"

Death, I think, but I never speak the word. I refuse to admit that my desire to coexist with the witches of Darkhaven has brought nothing but pain.

"There is good in the world, Papá," I say. "And it needs to be protected."

"There might be good, but there is also evil. There is darkness, and eventually, I learned to use it, to wield its power as my own."

"That's why you came back for me?" I ask, voice whisper soft.

The darkness. The amulet.

He nods.

"After I gained control, I was no longer its puppet," he

21

says. "I could think clearly, no longer driven by my blood lust, and I knew what I wanted to do. I sired others and taught them what I had learned."

He glances back at the rogue vampires, and they nod at him, an unspoken truth between them. Their gaze flickers to their leader for only a second before settling on me again. My pulse races despite my effort to remain calm, to look unruffled by the vampires around me.

"We are family now," my father says as he faces me again. "And I wanted you to see what I have created."

"You came back to kill me, didn't you?" I ask. Though I pose my thought as a question, I don't need validation. I already know his answer.

"I was surprised to learn that you already tasted this darkness. It had already claimed your soul, so I decided to watch you, to see how you handle the power it gave you. I watched as you learned to live with this darkness. You harnessed the very best parts of it, and you made a new family, just like I did."

"But I lost Mamá," I say. "By choosing the vampires, I lost the witches."

His face remains neutral. He does not confess that he is aware that my mother is dead, that our former coven is lost. He says nothing, even though I am certain he is somehow responsible. In Darkhaven, there are no coincidences. Mamá died after he came back, and I am sure he had something to do with it.

As much as I want to press on, to expose the truth in his heart, I don't. Because it's not time yet. I have to be smart about this. I must wait until the sun sets, until I am no longer trapped and outnumbered, with no means of escape.

"Mamá couldn't handle what I became," I continue. "She

cast me out of the coven, severing our ties."

"She was always weak," he says, voice hard.

"You say you came to kill me, to turn me into a vampire," I say. "What were your plans for her? And for *Abuela*?"

He smiles at the mention of his mother but shows no remorse for her death. Still, I think he knows what happened, how she died, that I am responsible.

He says he has been watching me, but I don't know for how long. I think about all the times the shadows bothered me, making my skin crawl, my senses jolt awake. Too often, I felt like I was being watched, only to find myself alone. How often was I wrong? How often was I *right*?

"I wanted us to be a family again, *hija*," he says. "But you were already a vampire. It saddened me to see that you did not fully appreciate this gift."

"You mean it upsets you that I have not willingly turned rogue."

He exhales sharply and curses under his breath. His patience is thinning, the line blurring between remaining a doting father and becoming a heartless demon. The monster within is waking, and I am the one holding the stick, using it poke after poke to irk an already irate beast.

I never knew I had such a staggering death wish.

Still, I continue, holding my ground as he dodges question after question.

"I have told you already," he says. "There are only mortals and immortals. There are humans and witches and vampires. Nothing more."

"There are humans who commit evil acts," I say. "There are witches who forsake their covens. It is entirely possible that not all vampires are the same. Some are evil, soulless creatures, and others are not."

His mouth curls into a sly grin, and I know I have played right into his hand. But it is too late to take back whatever secrets he thinks I have betrayed.

"Is that what happened?" he asks. "Tell me, *hija*, did they forsake you or did *you* forsake *them*?"

"I did my best to help them understand what it meant for me to become a vampire," I say. "I showed them that I am not rogue. Even after I transitioned, I was there for them. Where were you, Papá? Where were you when your family needed you?"

"I was there," he says. "But I didn't care about them. I was watching you."

"What happened to you?" I ask. "How did you become so callous, so apathetic toward the plight of your coven? I don't remember much from our time together before you died, but I know you were once a kind and caring man. What changed? What could you possibly have traded for your soul?"

"A soul is useless, Ava," he says. "A soul makes a man weak, so I traded it for the only thing worthwhile in this world. Raw, sheer, pure *power*."

The word drips from his lips like a stark, black promise, confirming what I feared were his true intentions for me, for the amulet I protect, for Darkhaven, for his rogue army.

Suddenly, it all makes sense. Every last word he has spoken has been a confession. He has given me the details I need to understand what happened to him all those years ago—and the truth of that night terrifies me. I swallow hard, the lump in my throat now the size of a boulder.

The more he speaks, the more he justifies his actions as being typical of a vampire, the more I am sure the hunters never lied to me. Amicia never lied to me. I believe that rogue vampires exist, that they are our common enemy.

But with this realization comes another startling truth.

Despite Papá's attempts to keep me in the dark, I learned something new today. My father is right. There are humans and witches and vampires, but the honesty of his statement ends there. What he didn't want me to realize is that I had the answers to my questions all along. Something else exists, and I have been speaking to it all day.

This creature is not merely a vampire nor is it simply a rogue. Like me—transforming into a hybrid that should not exist while I was on my deathbed—Papá died that day and evolved into something else, into something more powerful than any threat I have ever faced.

During this process—one that might have taken hours or days or even years—my father relinquished his soul in exchange for the power he so desperately sought. He told me that over time, he learned from this darkness, eventually taking control of the ancient evil, but I think he simply merged with it—much like the entity residing in my crystal wishes to do with me. If vampirism is a virus, then Papá has become its creator.

I want to believe that there is a chance that a small part of this creature might still be my father, but it is more likely he has been dead for a long time. The evil took control, and Papá was not strong enough to withstand it.

I think about the entity the witches summoned so many moons ago. I have kept it safely stored in my amulet, under my protection at all times. It dangles from my neck, stone cold and mute.

Ever since I made the decision to find this nest, to face the rogue vampires threatening the town's safety, the crystal has failed me, refusing to aid my call. The power has severed itself from me, and finally, no longer under its lure, I can think clearly.

As I stand before the creature that calls itself my father, the entity within the black onyx stone trembles.

FOUR

Exhaustion settles over me like the cool caress of the sea. It comes in waves, much like the water, and with each assault, I am sinking deeper into those dark depths. But rather than fearing the unknown, I find myself envying the sunken ship and the lost souls at the bottom of the gorge, because I yearn for the silence and serenity that comes with the deep.

The sea is merciless, consuming all in its path, but even a heartless mistress is a more favorable master than the rogue vampire who bears my father's face.

I tell myself that I must stay awake, that granting my weary body even a moment's peace will lead to certain death, but the promise of rest, inching closer with each passing second, has my troubled mind and steely determination waning. Each blink takes longer than the last, and even though I am terrified that once closed my eyelids will never reopen, I am eager for the wholesome revitalization that only comes from sleep.

Now, with several hours having passed since I discovered my father's secrets, I stand at the entrance to the cave, just far enough inside to avoid the sunlight beaming past me. The torridity of it webs toward me, threading through the darkness and writhing closer like billowing smoke. The heat is like thunder without lightning. It alone cannot hurt me, but that doesn't stop the warmth from gripping my neck like a noose. The fervor is suffocating, a promise of the sun's ultimate power over me, over us. I may not experience the juxtaposition of temperatures the way a human does, but I am well aware of its dire effects.

The echoing sound of the rogue army, nestled inside the belly of this labyrinth, vibrates off the slick walls. Slime coats each grunt, each annoyed hiss, each nauseating slurp of rotten human blood, and the moist smack of it corrodes my senses.

Still, I find myself listening intently, thinking about the vampires stationed here. I resent those who slumber, and I am nearly lulled to sleep by the mere sound of their steady breath. I envision their eyelids fluttering as they dream, whereas mine are becoming more paralyzed by the minute.

Even though I am closer to nightfall, closer to escaping this prison, I still feel no safer than I did when I first arrived. Everything around me feels like a nightmare, like a weapon that can be used against me—from the slippery ground to the rocky walls to the irritable rogues. I am on borrowed time, and the longer I stay here, the less of it I have.

I peer outside, shielding my eyes from the intense rays. The sweltering sun makes my skin sizzle, my nerves rapid-fire with admonition, and even though I know this is dangerous, I can't stop myself as I move closer to the entrance, skirting the line between light and dark, between life and death.

I have not experienced the midday sun since my transition. Only in my dreams—and sometimes in my nightmares— am I able to feel its rays penetrate my skin, to see the forest illuminated in such an invigorating light. Seeing it with fresh eyes, I am left awestruck by the world I no longer get to inhabit.

There is a soft dew covering the ground, making the

moss glisten like starlight. The fuzzy sparkle catches my eye, a glimmer in the daylight, and it twinkles, glowing brightly, as the brush twitches from movement.

Behind the mound, there is a rabbit. Its taupe-colored fur is speckled in dark markings. I can imagine running my fingers through the coarse texture, feeling its heartbeat against my palm. It ruffles through fallen twigs and decaying leaves to find sustenance, utterly unaware that it is in the presence of a hunter. Or maybe it knows I am here, and the sun has whispered assurances of my limitations.

The critter looks at me, beady eyes homing in on the entrance to the cave. Its mouth is full of greenery, with tiny stalks threaded through its gapped teeth, and it keeps an eye on me as I watch it eat. For a moment, it stills. We sit like this for several seconds, each waiting for the other to move. It breaks before I do. When it looks away, preoccupied with scavenging for more food, I know the sun has made it promises.

Squirrels are crawling up trees, skittering toward their massive nests. Some are brown, some black, some a startling red, and all have engorged cheeks, likely full from harvesting the new spring bounty. They move quickly, gazes darting around the forest, forever fearful of hawks and coyotes.

Branches are beginning to bud, and soon, the expansive treetops will be fleshy and green, full of life and vitality. I blink, and suddenly, I am a child again, running through the forest, arms outstretched as I trail the rough bark. The trunk scratches my fingertips, and I can still feel that tingle in my hand. I can still hear the soft hum of wind ruffling foliage, blowing leaves from where they perch.

Early spring flowers are in bloom, and the scent wafts closer. I inhale deeply, greedily, desperate to compare the smell to that of the night. But there is no comparison. The night is nothing like the day. It smells like shadows and death, dank and dreary, and the staunch terror of looming threats on all sides overpowers all-natural scents. Even the way one moves at night is different from those in the day. Nocturnal creatures are less carefree, less jovial.

Now that I stand at the edge of the entrance, taunting the sun with my very existence, I can see that the cave appears to be nestled in a steep hillside, close enough to the water for me to smell the salty sea air, to hear the waves splashing against rock. The vast, expansive forest that surrounds Darkhaven is before me, but when I squint through the trees, desperate to spot something familiar, I see nothing but endless green. When nightfall settles over this sleepy village, I will have no idea where to run or in what direction to trust is the right way home.

Already, I can practically taste the sweat seeping from hungry rogues as they track me. I can feel their breath as they are hot on my trail, tongues lapping my spilled blood as I tear through the forest, forgoing all sense of pride and wit. My escape from this prison will mean an abrupt, steadfast dash into the darkness, praying I remember enough of Mamá's lessons to find my way home. If I am to have any chance at all, I must remember everything she taught me about these woods and about the monsters that call them home.

I never knew this place existed, but Papá must have known it was here. I think he chose this cave as his lair because he knew I would never find him. The forest surrounding Darkhaven is like the sky. Regardless of how much time we spend exploring outer space, we still have only seen a small fraction of what is there. Even in all of my patrols, completed like clockwork every night, I never once ventured this far.

My assumption that he chose this place with the specific intention of avoiding being caught makes me wonder how long they have been here. How long has he been watching me? Has he seen my training sessions with Malik or intimate moments with Jasik? Has he seen me with Amicia or Will? Does he know I have access to magic? Like the universe, my questions are endless.

I think about Darkhaven. My hometown is a tiny, idyllic village that is barely a speck on any map. It is a beautiful place, with buildings lost in time. The scenery is breathtaking, a natural shield preventing others from finding us. The original settlers stumbled here hundreds of years ago, and since then, the town hasn't changed much. The houses are old, the streets are mainly cobblestone, and the people favor the mentality of keeping to themselves. This might be a picturesque place, definitely worthy of a top spot on the Best Of lists, but somehow, the sun sets and rises again without the arrival of outsiders. We remain in secrecy.

Yet in just a few weeks' time, there have been four newcomers.

First, there was the rogue vampire, who may or may not be tied to the assassination of my coven. It was a targeted attack, and the worst part is I am pretty sure they were coming for me. Except I wasn't there. So they took the only thing tethering me to my mortal life.

But if the death of my mother was at the hands of this particularly malicious rogue vampire, who sent him? Who told him how to find us?

Then there was the witch who claimed to be hunting the rogue vampire. She says he killed her coven, and in the name of vengeance, she planned to make him pay for upending her life. While I am partial to a good revenge plot, and I do appreciate that she protected my nest from the entity within the amulet during a time when I could not, I am still uncertain of her true intentions.

I want to like her. I really do. I want to trust that she is an ally, but every time she does something that should make me believe there is good in her, a blaring voice inside my heart screams at me to end her life before it is too late. Maybe it's my hunger. Maybe it's the darkness. Or maybe my instincts are right, and Sofía is up to no good.

With the fire causing the death of a dozen townspeople, the humans of Darkhaven became suspicious. This is a safe town. Arson is something seen on TV, not in our local paper. So they brought in new blood to uncover the truth behind that night. I understand their concern, but Jackson Griggs, the man investigating the fire, is a liability I cannot ignore. I like to think that even the animals of Darkhaven are on my side. Why else would the wolves attack him? Fortunately, he's a lucky man. He survived.

Now, my father is here—with an army to boot. He makes *four*. Four new arrivals in Darkhaven. Four strangers have settled here, and all of them can be tied to me. What is the likelihood of that? I have never been fond of math courses, but I am pretty certain the chances are slim.

Am I supposed to believe this is a coincidence? Am I supposed to trust that Papá has no connection to the witch or the rogue or the human? What about the dreamwalker? I need to ask my father about him, but I fear doing so will risk his life. I suppose I could count the dreamwalker as a fifth newcomer, but I haven't even proved that he exists.

The longer I stay here, the more I itch for freedom. I am well aware that I am dwindling into trepid imbecility. I feel eyes on me at every moment, and the continuous shudder that burrows its way through my limbs and up my spine is a painful reminder that *I am weak*. I am a lamb in the lions' den, a mortal on werewolf territory during the full moon.

I can trust no one—not the rogues who surround me, not even my father who raised me. I can barely trust myself.

My enemies are silent. Some slumber. Some busy themselves with mindless tasks. But some are watching me as I teeter the line between life and death, between light and dark.

The sun is shining brightly overhead, and many hours still separate me from my escape. I just have to wait. Waiting is the worst part. I have never been a patient person, and I am already exhausted, already feeling the tingling effect of hunger.

My stomach growls, but I pretend I do not hear it. I can risk no distraction. I cannot close my eyes, cannot turn my back on the others for long, cannot lose myself to my desire for food and rest.

It is getting darker now, and my limbs are heavy. I lean against the glossy, jagged wall. A thick drip of slime plops onto the nape of my neck, and it is soaked up by the collar of my jacket. My shirt is itchy and crinkly from dried sweat, and the odor from my body mixes with the pungent air in the cave.

A sharp ridge is nestled against the curve of my spine, but I welcome the stabbing pain as I continue to push against it, offering better angles to allow greater access. The ache in my back radiates through my bones, a dull torment that reminds me I am alive. I made it this far, and I can make it until sunset.

But the darkness is beginning to swallow me whole, inch by inch, piece by piece. It works its way up my legs, claiming my torso, my arms, my chest, and as it reaches my head, consuming my sanity, I know I am drifting to sleep.

With my eyes closed, I hear nothing but the silence punctuated by the firm, wet smacks of boots against the solid, rocky ground.

Someone is approaching, but I am already asleep.

FIVE

I open my eyes, and I am no longer in the cave. I am lying on my bed, staring at the ceiling. The milky-white color is blotchy and faded, and there are drips down the walls where the edges meet—clearly the brush strokes of a preteen child.

The fan overhead is on, and the soft swooshing sends a rush of cool air down on me. My skin prickles and I shiver, but I do not move. I do not close my eyes, because if I do, I fear I may lose my grasp on this memory. And I don't want to go back.

I inhale deeply, the familiar scent of incense filling my nose. I relish the aroma, gulping breath after breath until my lungs spasm. The house smells like sage and lavender, and it feels safe and warm. The threat of vampires and feuds and death are the last things on my mind, as is the sadness of losing my father. In this memory, I still miss him—the hole in my heart making that painfully clear—but little by little, day by day, losing him is getting easier. I spent my nights praying to see him again, but I never tricked myself into believing it was actually possible, that wishes and good intentions alone could really bring him back.

I sit upright and scoot back until I can lean against the headboard. My blankets are bunched at my knees, so I kick them off. I am wearing shorts and a loose-fitting T-shirt. My skin is bronzed, my legs covered in bruises and scrapes. I wiggle my toes, hissing as I do so. My big toe is broken, but the swelling has decreased. I think I can walk on it again. But I am not ready to stand, so I continue assessing my former bedroom.

The curtains are drawn, and daylight streams through, illuminating what should be a darkened space. I welcome the warmth, but the rays do not eliminate the chill. It still manages to settle deep in my bones, an internal ache I may never sate. If there is one thing I have learned since my transition, it is that humanity is one spectacular agony after another—all made bearable by mundane senses.

My bedroom door is closed, but I can still hear the muffled sounds coming from downstairs. There is music and humming, each syllable a soft caress to my ears.

These are the moments I miss. It's the small things people take for granted that I can never get back, like when Mamá would sneeze so loud I swear the walls shook or when she would practice English by saying the same thing twice—once in both languages. I miss her stillness in the way she would watch the birds or the way she spoke to her plants as though they could hear her. I miss the way she would speak to our ancestors by walking through the cemetery. That's why having my own memorial site right outside the manor is so important to me.

As I sit on the bed that no longer exists, having been reduced to ash by fire, my heart swells. I remember this day in vivid detail, and even though I *know* this is a dream, everything about it feels *real*.

Once again, I am a young girl, a *mortal*—thirteen years old—and Mamá hasn't completely lost herself to her bitterness. She was kinder back then, more hopeful about my future in the coven and the promise of what that meant. Her pain over losing Papá in such brutal fashion has eased a bit, allowing her to breathe. Finally, she stopped searching for his face in a crowd of people, stopped waiting for him to walk through the door like nothing ever happened.

Rather than rush downstairs to greet her, I scan the photos on my wall—each image a prominent moment in time, each marking decisions that affected our lives irrevocably.

The frames are mismatched, the staging off center, the lining of each section crooked. The untrained eye might see a disheveled mess, but I see organized chaos. I remember beaming up at the collage after I finished, never feeling prouder than I did in that moment. It took weeks of me painstakingly flipping through photo albums until I found the exact pictures I wanted to use, and for a preteen, weeks can feel like a lifetime.

There are five. Five perfect moments, captured forever by the single click of a camera shudder. Each one a tick in time.

The first is of my parents. In it, they are teenagers, young and in love. They stand side by side, their carefree smiles wide and true. My mother is looking at someone behind the camera, and her smile is warped in a way that tells me she was about to speak or maybe laugh. My father is looking at my mother, a sparkle in his eyes. I like to think this is the moment he fell in love with her—the *exact* second—and it was caught on camera. That's what I love about this photo. It makes me want to be lighthearted and untroubled, like only the young can be.

The second picture is from their wedding day. My father is standing behind my mother, his arms cocooning her body against his. My mother is cradling her stomach. My father's hands are cupping my mother's, and they are looking into each other's eyes. Something there, within that glimmer of hope that is glowing between them, tells me they are keeping a secret. I think she is pregnant with me, and no one else knows. No one but her and him and me.

The third photo is of my birth. My mother is lying on a bed. Her hair is bedraggled, her eyes sunken and tired. Her skin is pale but plump. Her cheeks are rosy from exertion, her forehead pebbled with sweat. And even with all of this, from her unkempt appearance to the damp and rumpled bedsheets, she has never looked happier or more beautiful. My father is standing beside her, leaning over. He is kissing her head, but she is paying him no attention. I am wrapped in a soft-pink blanket and cradled in her arms. Tears are streaking down her cheeks, soaking the wrapping she put me in. No one is looking at the camera.

The fourth image was taken while my father was building our home. I am standing in the yard, picking wildflowers while wearing a white, billowing dress that moves with the wind. I am a toddler, maybe two or three, and I have a hand full of weeds. But I am smiling as I look at my mother, who is taking the photo. A few yards away, my father is measuring wood planks as he builds the frame of our house.

The final snapshot is of my initiation into the coven, when I was old enough to participate in rituals. My hair was tied back into a tight braid, and it is dangling down my spine. I am wearing a burgundy cloak, and Abuela is pointing a dagger at my throat. I have one foot lifted, as if in step, to enter the circle. I was terrified that day, overly fearful that I would mess up my lines or drop my offering. I never once thought about vampires, about how one simple request would alter my life forever.

When I stand, I walk to my dresser and stare at my reflection in the mirror that is hanging on the wall above it.

I notice a few glaring differences. My inky-black hair is still long and smooth, the tresses the color of the starless night sky, but my eyes are no longer crimson. They are the shade of dark wood, brown and murky. My skin, no longer pale and perfect, is tan and scraped with fresh wounds. During my teenage years, I made my vow to protect my coven, and I spent my nights dueling with whoever would train me. Most times, Liv was the only volunteer. She would cast fireballs for me to dodge—a few coming so close my hair would catch fire.

I think about Liv for a long time before I finally move away from the mirror and complete my morning routine, showering and dressing, like a puppet controlled by its master. These are the same actions I completed that day, and even though my elemental control over spirit grants me the power to change this, I don't. I find strength and comfort in completing these tasks, in being *normal*.

When I grasp the doorknob, twisting until the latch frees, a surge of excitement courses through me. I step into the hallway and glance in each direction. To my right are the stairs that will lead me to the first story. To my left is a row of other closed doors—one leading to Mamá's bedroom, another leading to a guest room, and the final leading to our altar room.

I descend to the first floor, taking the steps two at a time. I plop onto the bottom landing in a thud, my ankles protesting the abrupt halt. The front door is to my right, the living room in front of me, and the hallway that leads to the rest of the house is to my left.

I turn and walk toward the kitchen, peering into the empty living room and attached dining room. I pass the hall closet that leads to the basement, pausing slightly as an involuntary shudder permeates through my spine. I do not open that door.

I enter the kitchen, and I see her. All at once, time slows.

Her hair, streaked with gray, is pulled up into a tight bun, with loose strands dangling to her shoulders. She is still dressed in her night clothes, covering them with an apron tied in a bow behind her back. She is barefoot and has reading glasses perched atop her head. She yawns loudly and teeters from foot to foot.

Her back is to me as she makes breakfast. She hums softly to the soothing sounds of instrumental music, completely unaware of my presence. For a moment, I let myself believe she won't see me even when she turns around, and the thought makes my heart sink. Because I want her to see me. I want her to assure me that she's okay, that the pain and confusion caused by the entity's influence are gone. I need to know that she doesn't blame me for her death, even though my curse is what left her vulnerable to an attack.

I take a single step forward, the floorboards creaking under my weight, and my mother spins around, gasping at the sight of me.

"*Me asustaste*," she says, breathy and unnerved.

She clutches her chest, managing to swipe the dirty spatula she was using across the front of her apron. An orange streak of melted cheese stains the white fabric, with loose strings now connecting her chest to the utensil.

"Mamá," I say, voice whisper soft. "*Te he echado de menos.*"

I tell her I have missed her, but I know she won't understand. She won't even hear the confession because I didn't say this back then. I didn't miss her the way I do now. I took for granted the fact that she was always here, always ready to greet me in the morning.

"¿Tienes hambre?" she asks.

I don't respond, even though I am hungry. My stomach grumbles in response, and she laughs.

"*Buena*," she says, answering me as she did all those years ago. "*Siéntate.*"

I obey and move to the kitchen table to sit down. The last time I sat here, I felt like a zombie. I had just been cursed by my coven. That was when Will was alive, when my coven committed the ultimate betrayal. So much has changed since that moment. So much has happened that I swore I would never forgive. But the longer I stare at my mother, the more I realize the grace in forgiveness. She might deserve punishment for her actions, but she did what she thought was right. She only wanted to save my soul. I just wish I could go back and tell her it was her soul that needed saving.

"It's going to rain today," I say mindlessly.

I am not looking outside. My gaze never even leaves my mother. But I know it will rain, and I know she and I will talk about the weather. Because that's what happened before, when this was real.

Like clockwork, my mother glances out the window above the sink, leaning forward to get a clear view. Her apron becomes soaked at the chest by the water in the sink where dishes are waiting to be scrubbed, but she doesn't react to the mess, even as it seeps into her nightgown.

She nods when she sees the overcast sky.

"We will still complete your lessons," she says.

I sigh and draw squiggly circles on the table with my fingers. I didn't think it was possible to feel worse about losing her, but seeing her now, unable to communicate properly, brings back the pain, intensifying it tenfold.

A single tear escapes my restraint. It drips down my

cheek and splashes against the tabletop. The droplet magnifies the grain and the natural yellow tint of the oak wood. I don't bother wiping it away.

"Yes," my mother says. "But you must complete your studies first."

She is speaking to me, responding to questions I asked years ago. I remember them all. I remember this exact conversation. It is burned into my memory, like all the rest. The cruelty of time is that I can remember all these little moments with Mamá, who wasn't always kind to me, but the moments I had with Papá, who was much more supportive, are fading. I lost him when I was too young to remember the good over the bad, and it was the bad, the thoughts of how he died and by what hand, that fueled my desire to contribute to the fruitless war against vampires.

"*Se está haciendo tarde*," my mother says, continuing her one-sided conversation. "Eat quickly, *hija*."

"Yes, Mamá," I say.

She puts a plate of chorizo and eggs in front of me. She walks away but returns with a glass of orange juice. I stare at the plate, stomach growling but knowing this will not sate my hunger. Still, I yearn to please her—even if I know the task is moot.

Sighing heavily, I pick up the fork and stab a mound of eggs. The metal scrapes against the ceramic dish, the screeching sound echoing off the walls.

My mother's hand settles over mine, and her grip tightens. I suck in a sharp breath, hissing her name. This is new. This did not happen then. I try to pull away, but she does not release me.

I meet her gaze, but her vision is lost. Her eyes are glossed over, and her jaw ticks, the tiny muscles bulging as she bites down hard. Her head jerks to the left over and over again, small, sharp movements that make her look like a malfunctioning robot.

"Mamá?" I say softly.

She does not respond.

Her grip is hard, so taut she could break bones. Her nails dig into my flesh, but my skin does not break. Because this isn't supposed to happen. She didn't cut me then, so she shouldn't be able to harm me now. Still, I am fearful of what she might do.

Her body stiffens as her head continues to lurch to the side. I stare in disbelief, unsure of what to do or what to say to calm her. My skin is burning where her flesh meets mine, and my heart is beating so loudly, it matches her convulsions.

"Mamá!" I shout. "You're hurting me."

She stops. Her grip loosens, but she does not release me.

"Ava," she whispers. Her voice is warped with pain.

"*Está bien*, Mamá," I say, my gaze on her unmoving hand.

I am breathing heavily now, and my mind is reeling from what just happened. This is not the first time I have dreamed of the past, but never before has my dream strayed from truth. Deviation only occurs in my nightmares. And this is not a nightmare.

I look up at her when she begins to rub the pad of her thumb against my skin, tracing the outline of invisible hearts. Her eyes are filled with tears, and she is smiling at me.

"My Ava," she says, and I know I am no longer dreaming of that day. We have been transported, with the spirit element guiding our souls, to the astral plane, where her soul has waited for mine.

The barrier of our former home falls away, and we are

surrounded by vast openness, like the infinite outer space. The air is misty, with the fog settling low. I can see only a few feet in front of me, but that's enough. Because that's where she is.

"Mamá," I say, voice squeaky.

She pulls me close, arms wrapping protectively around my body. She feels warm against my cooler frame. We are the same height, so I rest my head in the crook of her neck, and I inhale deeply. She smells like nothing, because she is *nothing*. She is empty space taking the form of someone I know, someone I love. Just like my father.

I flinch at the thought, momentarily paralyzed by my fear.

What if this isn't real? What if I'm not dreaming and this is some sick game *he* is playing?

"*Vas a estar bien*," Mamá says, as if she can hear my internal apprehension. "You are okay now."

"I've missed you," I confess.

My innards are still riddled with anxiety, but the truth of my words cuts through the tangles. I don't remember a time I ever had a good relationship with my mother, but that doesn't mean I don't regret my actions—many of which that led to her death. She didn't deserve to die. Especially not by the hands of a maniac rogue vampire.

"*Yo también te extraño*," she says. "I have missed you very much."

My mother is holding me so tightly, I almost can't breathe. She rocks side to side, teetering between her feet, and I move with her, letting the motion soothe my pain and guilt and doubt.

When I close my eyes, I can almost feel her as she once was—warm and vibrant, strong and supreme. And I can almost smell the earthy aroma of her perfume. But the longer

I hold on to the past, the more I overuse my memory muscle, and the exertion is making me drowsy. The ability to feel tired while sleeping is the curse of a spirit user. Sometimes I wake more exhausted than when I went to bed.

"He's back, Mamá," I say, knowing we haven't the time to dance around the subject.

She stills, arms a steel barrier around my torso. Her hands are stiff, and they cling tightly to my body. Although I know it's impossible, I swear I can feel her skin cooling, like the news alone has made her lethargic. She is trembling, the jitters making my own bones rattle.

"¿Qué pasó, Mamá?" I ask.

She pulls away abruptly, holding me at an arm's length. Her fingers curl around my flesh, nails biting into my skin. She squeezes, hard, as if she must inflict pain to ensure I am giving her every ounce of my attention. Eyes wide and unblinking, I do not dare look away.

"Mamá?" I say, breathlessly.

"You must listen to me, *mija*," she warns. "You are in danger. This is why I came back to you."

"Is it Papá?" I ask.

I speak in a whisper, ever mindful that my body is still in the cave. Physically, I am vulnerable to him, and I worry about what that truly means. Can he reach me here? Is he powerful enough to step into my dreams?

"*Ese no es tu padre*," she says, seething.

She tightens her grip, and I suck air through my clenched jaw. The hissing sound is loud, and it penetrates the space around us.

"What is he?" I ask, dreading every syllable of my question.

I didn't want it to come to this. As much as I feared him, as uneasy as I felt around him, I still wanted to believe he was my father.

She opens her mouth to speak, but she is soundless. She tries again, still painfully mute. She releases me and grabs her throat, but her voice is paralyzed. She cannot speak. She cannot warn me.

Her eyes betray her fear, growing wide and dark. Tears pool in the corners as she overexerts herself. Her skin is becoming pale, and I think she cannot even breathe. Something harrowing passes between us, a staggering jolt, and she is ripped away from me. Gone, in an instant.

I believe I am alone, left to the astral plane, the ample nothingness, but then he speaks.

The echo of his voice pierces the silence in this place. I do not see him, but I know he is here.

"You are in danger," he says, mirroring my mother's earlier words.

"Mamá?" I shout, ignoring the dreamwalker's warning.

"You must get rid of the amulet before it is too late," he continues, tone hard, commanding.

"Mamá!" I shout.

I let myself believe the sheer panic in my voice is enough to lure her back to me. But I know it is not. She is gone now, and I am alone with the dreamwalker.

"You are running out of time."

His words are meant to caution, but they linger like a threat.

SIX

I jolt awake, gasping as I sit upright. I plunge into consciousness, releasing the astral plane as my soul settles, my skin wrapping around my essence like a coil.

The subtle uneasiness of being watched begins to rise in my chest, like bile moving up my gut. The taste is sour, the smell rancid, and I gag, chest heaving as I struggle to breathe while inhaling the odor.

Returning from the astral plane is a jarring experience. Everything feels like it's just out of reach. My limbs are heavy, my grasp weak. I grab hold of something just to watch it slip through my fingers. It feels like I am in neither place—not the spiritual plane nor the physical one—and yet it feels like I'm in both places at the same time, with one foot resting on both sides of the invisible line. It is both bizarre and extraordinary, and even though I rely much less on my magical heritage than I used to, I am grateful I can still tap into this power.

I lean against the slimy, rocky wall to assess my surroundings. I am dangerously close to the light spilling inside the cave. Slowly, as the sun begins to set, the stream is moving farther away from me. But even as the sun sinks behind the horizon, its power is no less deadly. I was one nightmare and a quick body thrust away from a really bad day.

My skin is tingling, hairs prickling as I scan the small

entrance. Everything looks the same. I am still trapped here, surrounded by rogue vampires. I am still hours away from my freedom. But I do feel different. The ominous warning from both the dreamwalker and my mother loops in my mind. It too coils around my body like skin, but the dreamwalker's words are starting to tighten around my chest, transforming to a vise-like grip in a matter of seconds. The pressure is becoming too much to bear.

The vampire claiming to be my father is watching me. He is perched on a rock ledge a few feet away. Like me, he rests just within the safety of the darkness. He smiles when our gazes meet, a hint of deviance sparkling behind his blood-red irises.

"You were dreaming," he says, voice smooth, tone almost comforting.

But it's the words he chooses *not* to say that are unmistakable.

You were asleep, and I chose not to kill you. You should trust me now.

But I know I can't trust him. I don't believe he protected me during a vulnerable moment because he *wanted* to. I think he *had* to. Because he needs me. Just not in the way I yearn for. I want him to need me because I am his daughter, not because I am a hybrid vampire with a powerful—and possibly defunct—amulet at my collarbone. I resist the urge to grasp the stone, preferring his interest stay on *me* rather than the crystal.

"What do you dream?" he asks.

I frown. His tone, soft and sincere, marks his question as a true query, like he has never before experienced a dream so he truly doesn't understand the concept. He doesn't phrase it in a way that is singular—*what do* you *dream about?*—he asks it as though everyone sees the same pictures when they close their eyes. But we don't. He should know that. He might be a monster now, but he was once mortal. He once lived for his dreams.

I shrug. "Probably the same things you dream about."

"I don't dream," he says simply.

"Never?" I ask, unbelieving. "You must dream when you sleep."

"I rarely sleep," he says. "When I do, I see nothing. It is blank and black, and then I wake again."

I think about his confession, letting the words settle deep before I respond. I find it strange that he doesn't dream. Even while under the influence of the entity, I still had dreams—though they often morphed into nightmares. But when I closed my eyes at night, I was not greeted by darkness.

"I dreamed about Mamá," I say, choosing honesty.

I watch him carefully, reading his emotional response. I want to see if his eyes narrow, if his nose twitches, if his lips purse at the mention of his late-wife. I want to see if he blinks too long or not enough, if he rolls his eyes or snorts.

But he does none of these things. He simply nods, intrigued by my admission. He actually looks ... *interested*. Like he is generally pleased with my response. I choose to believe him. If dreaming is a foreign concept to him, he probably really is enjoying this conversation.

"I also dreamed about a witch," I say, treading the very fine line between ousting and protecting.

I don't clarify *which* witch. I don't tell him that the dreamwalker is still contacting me, urging me to destroy the amulet. I don't admit this because I am still convinced my father knows more about him than I do. The fact that the witch is still contacting me makes me believe my father is unaware of his ability to reach me, so the last thing I want to do is put him in danger.

But I need information. I need to know if he's okay or if he is also imprisoned here, captive to the sun or detained by the vampires. Perhaps both are accurate. Maybe this dreamwalker isn't a witch at all. Maybe he's a hybrid.

I wait for a response, but my father does not react. He simply stares at me, as though *he* is waiting for *my* explanation.

"Are we alone?" I ask.

He shakes his head. "*Sabes que no estamos solos.*"

"Who else is here?" I say, desperately trying to keep my voice calm.

My heart is racing, and I am lightheaded. I can't decide if my reaction is to him or because of my hunger. My stomach grumbles, and we both hear it. He glances at my gut, eyes sparkling before returning to my gaze.

"There are vampires here, *hija*," he says, continuing our conversation. "You know this."

"Yes, but is there a witch here?" I clarify. "Is there a witch somewhere in this cave?"

He is silent for a moment, the seconds ticking by more like hours. He furrows his brow, a confused look splashed across his face. His gaze trails my body, from tousled hair to scuffed boot. He looks at me like I am speaking a foreign language and he believes the clues in understanding my questions are hidden in my demeanor.

"No," he says finally. "There is no witch here. There are only vampires."

I am silent, slowly digesting his response, but something deep down is eating away at me. Mamá returned from the afterlife to warn me, claiming this man is not my father. She fears I am in danger, and if that is true, Papá is somehow involved.

He must know the witch I am asking about. He has to. He insists there is no one else here except for the two of us and the rogue army, but someone helped guide me to this place. Someone entered the astral plane with the sole purpose of warning me about impending danger. If I am to stay true to my belief that there are no such things as coincidences in Darkhaven, then I have to believe Papá is involved. And if he is involved, he may be the reason my life is in danger. Worse yet, he could be the *cause*.

As I think about everything that has happened in just a few days, I fidget with the black onyx crystal, but what was once warm and tingly, reacting to my mere touch, is silent and void of power. Ever since I met my father, the darkness has hidden, choosing isolation and confinement to freedom and absolute power.

When my father returns to me, having left momentarily, granting me several minutes of peace, he brings a human with him. The boy is young, maybe ten. His blond hair is stringy from sweat, and his blue eyes are pooled with tears. He shivers when I meet his gaze—from the sight of me or from the cold, I'm unsure. He is shirtless, wearing only jeans, but the fabric of his pants is shredded, offering minimal coverage on this cool spring day.

His skin is scraped and raw, his nails caked with dirt. Dried streams of crimson streak down his neck, coating his shoulder with blood. There are puncture marks down his arms, where scabs are beginning to form. I don't know how long he has been here, tormented and enslaved, but I think it's been days. Maybe longer.

My father is holding him upright with a hand to the back of his neck. When he releases the boy, the child falls, unable to carry his own weight. His legs buckle, and his knees smack against the ground. A loud crack permeates the otherwise silent space between us. He yelps, curling on to his side to cradle his wound.

I rise quickly, the smell of the boy wafting closer. It surrounds me, the tantalizing aroma of blood consuming my thoughts. My stomach gurgles, and my instincts take over. My fangs throb, my heart races, but the fog in my mind clears, my gaze pinpointing the exact spot I can easily access the child's blood supply. His veins are pulsating, rushing his life essence through his body at invigorating speeds.

Everything about this boy welcomes me to take his life, making me want to indulge—just once—in what it means to be a vampire.

And that is exactly why Papá brought him here, when it is nearly dusk, when I am weak from hunger and exhaustion and not able to think clearly. He thought I would be too weak to resist, but he was wrong.

"Taste him," he says.

I refuse. My stomach reacts painfully, squeezing so tightly I think I might buckle over, joining the child on the ground.

"You must feed," he says sternly.

"I would rather die," I hiss.

"You will," he says. "You must eat, or you will die. Why is his life more important than yours?"

"He is innocent," I say.

"But you have the power to do more. You can spend several lifetimes committing the good acts you so boldly seek, whereas he has only one life to live. Choosing death for yourself and life for him makes no sense. Don't you see that?"

"No good deed I commit will be worth anything if a river of blood follows in my wake," I say.

He sighs heavily and runs a hand through his hair. The setting sun casts an eerie glow against his skin, making him look infernal and crazed. His eyes are sunken, the bright blood-red color almost neon beside his translucent skin. His cheek bones are pronounced. The curious tilt of his head only makes them look sharper and more angular.

"Can I offer you another?" he asks. "Perhaps its age is what bothers you."

I don't miss how he refers to this child as an *it*. No matter what I say, he will never understand. Monsters are incapable of empathizing with anyone who isn't evil.

"Let me make this perfectly clear," I begin. "I am not like you. I will *never* be like you, and frankly, I wouldn't even trust a blood bag if it was offered by your hand."

He smiles. "There's my girl. So strong and confident. You were always this way. Your mother never appreciated these qualities, but I did."

I cringe when he mentions my mother.

"I am *not* your girl," I say, jaw clenched.

"You are that and so much more, *hija*," he says. "You are the very best parts of me. You are the pieces I am missing, the ones I need."

I narrow my gaze at him, remaining silent long enough for him to decide the fate of the boy on his own.

"You say there is a lack of trust," he says. "Well, I shall show you that you can trust me, that you can trust the sustenance I offer."

He grabs the boy's arm, lifting him clean off the ground so that he dangles in the air by his limb. The child fights back, clawing at his captor with his only free hand. He uses his fist, but nothing happens. The rogue doesn't even flinch. What the boy hasn't yet realized is that mortals stand no chance against immortals.

With drool seeping down his chin, my father licks his lips and then snarls as he tears into the child's flesh. His victim screams, a soul-piercing cry that shreds every ounce of my heart. I decide then that I will save him—at all costs.

I lunge forward, striking the back of my hand against my father's cheekbone. I hoped it would derail him long enough to release the boy. This doesn't happen. Instead, I am the one who feels pain. A sharp cramp shoots through my wrist and down my arm. The force of my assault felt like stick against steel, and the tiny prickle in my hand informs me I nearly broke a bone.

My father doesn't even flinch, but his surprise and anger are enough to make him stop. With pink-stained fangs bared, he pulls away from his victim, so I attack again. This time, I thrust the palm of my hand upward, smacking his jaw closed and thrusting his head backward. The force of my blow sends him stumbling back, but only a few inches. Still, it's enough for him to release the child.

The human falls, and I grab onto him, pulling his frail body into my arms. I hold him close, but not too tight, as I stumble backward, putting as much space between my father and us as I can.

In my arms, the child bleeds out, slowly but steadily. I can feel the heat of his blood cascading down my arm. His heart is hammering against my chest, a rapid-fire difference compared to my own fierce beats. He keeps his body curled against mine, head resting against the curve of my neck. I feel his tears as they soak my shirt, but the sensation is nothing compared to the way he holds me. He digs his fingers into my clothes, clinging desperately to the one vampire intent on sparing him.

"You're going to be okay," I whisper, but I think he can't hear me over his loud sobs.

My father regains his composure and snarls at us. He dashes forward, but I am already at the entrance. I am one step away from the light, from the protection the sun will provide the boy.

I step into it, and I am lit aflame.

The intensity of the sun is not what I expected—it's worse. The heat alone is excruciating, the fever making it difficult to breathe. My lungs, unaware that this is a losing battle, fight to consume oxygen, but I am already drowning; my organs are already liquefying.

I scream as my skin ignites in blisters. It takes only seconds for the boils to burst, resulting in acidic pus to seep down my body, leaving gashes in its wake.

I hear my father scream my name, but I keep walking, taking one agonizing step at a time, until I cannot any longer.

I fall to my knees, the rough smack of my kneecaps resonating deep in my bones, and I drop the boy before he too catches fire. He tumbles from my arms, rolling away. As I cower on all fours, he looks at me, scooting away on his behind. He doesn't stop until he backs into a tree, and by then, he is so far, no vampire will reach him. Not until the sun sets.

"Run!" I shout, summoning all of my energy into the one

word, but my voice cracks, the order a whisper.

The boy is crying, and I think he thanks me, but I am already falling to the ground, face plummeting into the cool, moist earth. The soil burrows around my body as I slam into it, but before I am greeted by the sweet caress that only death can offer me, I am being hurled backward, flung into the cave's dark depths.

My father is pinning me against the wall, jabbing my spine into the protruding rocks. I grunt, but the stabbing agony in my back is nothing compared to the all-consuming pain of my sizzling skin. The sound of my charred flesh is everywhere, and the smell is like nothing I have ever experienced. The pungent odor of my melting flesh consumes all of my senses. I can hear nothing else. I can *taste* nothing else. I can feel *nothing else.*

Until my boils begin to heal, and I realize my father's clenched hand is wrapped around my throat. His fingers have sunk into my flesh, and I am bleeding. I wince as he squeezes tighter, cursing under my breath.

"You live your life as a caged animal, Ava," he says, voice dark and stern. "It's really rather disappointing."

I try to speak, but my voice is still lost. I choke out a breath, and my vision begins to blur.

"You were prepared to offer your life in exchange for his," he says, shaking his head.

He loosens his grip just enough for me to respond, but he speaks before I can.

"Do you know how disappointing that is?" he asks. "You're my child, my protégé."

"I told you," I say, the sound wet between my teeth. "I am *nothing* like you."

This time, he nods and exhales sharply.

"I suppose you're right," he says. "You are not like me. You are weak, and I am only interested in power."

SEVEN

As the sun begins to dip below the horizon, I know I am only minutes away from freedom. I stand near the entrance, ready to dash into the forest as soon as the light poses no threat. I even consider leaving now, but I am not sure I would heal from another assault. Even dusk risks further exposure.

I need to be smart about my escape. I can afford zero mistakes. I am weak and outnumbered, and the sleeping rogues will soon rise. If they find me before I reach the manor, survival is unlikely. And with me gone, there will be no one to warn the hunters or the town.

The boy will speak about his time in this cave, but as soon as he mentions vampires, psychologists will argue his imagination is a coping mechanism to help him recover from what he endured. They will say the brain is a magnificent organ; it can make one believe just about anything. That might be true, but this time, the threat of vampires is real.

Woozy from hunger and exhaustion, I wobble on my feet, bracing myself by placing my hand on the greasy wall so I don't tumble over. As the sun sets, the temperature drops, and the water dripping down the cavern's rock walls is turning icy. I don't lower my arm because I like the bitter sensation against my palm.

Even though the cold can't harm me, it still makes my

skin prickle. It's an evolutionary trait I am glad I didn't lose when I became immune to things like frostbite. Because even though I won't die from the frigid air, I still want to experience as much as I can in the same way mortals do. It makes me feel . . . *normal.*

Papá approaches from behind. I don't look at him, but I know he is there. I feel his presence against my skin, that subtle shift in the air. It affects me just like the cold. The tiny hairs all over my body are alerted, some nearly standing on end in response.

He doesn't hide his approach. I can even hear him breathing, loud and perverted. The suction of his lungs filling with air makes a nauseating sucking sound with each inhalation, causing my skin to crawl, a shudder of disgust washing over me. I can smell him too, and he smells like death—like sour milk and spoiled meat. I thought I might get used to the stink of this place, but after spending the day here, the stench remains.

Even with him treading closer, I keep my sight on the forest ahead. Slowly, my vision is adjusting to the encroaching darkness. I ready myself by arching the ball of my foot against the jagged earth, prepared to propel myself forward, into the darkness and far from this cave. I tell myself I will make it, that I am faster than any rogue army. I will survive this night, and I believe the lie. For a brief second, I think this will work. I trust that I will make it home unscathed.

"Ava," my father says.

His voice is rough and deep, his accent hearty and robust. I shiver in response because I know he is close behind me. My instincts are kicking in, shouting at me to flee or fight, but I do neither. I remain still, steadying my breath so Papá believes he holds no power over me.

"I have no intention of keeping you here after the sun has set," my father says.

"I don't believe you," I admit.

I keep my voice calm, trusting I can fool him with reserved demeanor. I'm sure I am failing spectacularly, but I trudge forward nonetheless. I refuse to be the only uneasy vampire in his cave. I just hope my confidence throws him off his game—whatever that may be.

"You are of no use to me if kept against your will," he says.

"You no longer need me, do you?" I ask. "Did I foil your plan because I am not the soulless monster you hoped for?"

He chuckles and walks closer, walking through a puddle as he steps directly behind me. The moist suction of his boot absorbing the water makes me cringe, but the sound is nothing compared to his funky breath hot on my neck.

"Of course I need you, *hija*," he says. "I came back for you *because* I need you."

"Sorry you came all this way for such a disappointment," I say, voice deadpan.

"In time, you will learn that you can trust me," he says. "You can believe what I tell you because I have no reason to lie. I have only your best interests at heart."

I snort, the abrupt crash of my grunt in such a silent space louder than I intended. I curse internally. The last thing I want to do is upset him. If he really is offering me a peaceful exit, then I must take it. It might be my only chance to avoid battling his army.

"I understand your hesitance," he says. "But I do hope you will choose to return to me of your own free will."

I turn my back on the setting sun so I can face the vampire

who bears a striking resemblance to me. I once had his eyes, from the almond shape to the chestnut color, but now mine are bright crimson and his are a somber ruby. I still have his sharp nose and his angular eyebrows. Even our skin is the same pale shade, and as he towers over me, the space between us dangerously close, I see myself in the mischievous glint he has. I don't particularly like seeing any version of myself in a rogue vampire, especially one who claims to be my father.

Mamá is certain that this vampire is not Papá. I suppose she should know. She spent more time with him than I did. She had decades when I only had years. She believes he is *el diablo*—evil incarnate—and that he came for my soul. This is probably true, and even though I trust her more than I will ever trust him—and considering everything *she* did to me, that alone should be more than enough for me to sever ties— the little girl in me, who is faced with an eternity orphaned, is praying this man is her father. She hopes even the damned can be saved. But the realist in me is prepared to drive a stake through his heart.

I stare at him, taking in all of his features as though this will be the last time I will ever see my father in physical form. I know it won't be. As he wishes, I will return to him. Because if my father—my *real* father—offered his soul to whatever evil controls him now, then I shall get it back for him. Freeing him will be my revenge.

But first, I must know how far gone he truly is.

"Mamá is dead," I say.

He knows I am testing him, and he does not respond, doesn't move at all. He waits for me to continue.

"Our entire coven has been murdered," I add. "Do you know anything about that?"

He shakes his head, unspeaking, but his silence is deafening. I can hear nothing else over my boiling anger. My frustration is rising, and Papá is testing the very little patience I possess.

When the moments trickle on, with both of us refusing to speak first, he finally breaks. I consider this a profound win.

"I came back for you—*only you*," he says. "I do not care about the others."

"What about your mother?" I ask. "Do you not care for Abuela, the woman who offered you life?"

"She served her purpose," he says plainly.

His lack of emotions is not only starting to irk me, they are also leaving me rather unsettled. Only the soulless can be so crass.

I take a single step forward, completely closing the space between us. Since this day began, we have been playing a game of chess, a battle of wits, each making small, intentional moves toward a deadly conclusion. Now, we wait to see who can claim *checkmate* first. My final move in tonight's game is a show of dominance. I am challenging his leadership. He is an alpha to this pack of rogues, and I assume he won't take kindly to being challenged when he should have home field advantage.

Amusement flickers behind his eyes. Earlier, he said he appreciates my stubborn personality, likely even my rash demeanor. He once praised it for being some of my very best qualities. Tonight, I intend to see how far that appreciation goes.

"Did you kill my mother?" I ask.

I do not break eye contact. I wait, standing my ground, prepared to see the question through. Even if I am surrounded by rogues, body being torn to shreds, I will not fall first. He says he came back for me, but I am not the mortal daughter he left behind. I am a hybrid, one foot planted firmly in both worlds, and he will experience just how powerful I truly am.

"No, *mija*," he says. "I did not."

"Did you order someone to kill her?" I continue.

"No," he says, after a moment's hesitation.

Only one single second passed before he responded, but that delay is enough to frazzle my emotions.

He tried to remain calm when he spoke. His voice did not crack. His eyes remained focused. His pulse did not change. But I know he is lying. He hesitated, and somehow, I *know* he was involved.

Before I became a vampire, I might have responded by lunging without thinking, without considering that a fight now will lead to death but a battle later can result in victory. The hunters would be proud. If they have taught me nothing else, they have trained me to be strategic. I might make a lot of mistakes and lead with my heart over my head, but this time, I intend to win.

I will avenge my mother, release my father, and slay the demon controlling his body.

But now isn't the time, so I retreat and wait for the darkness to find me again.

EIGHT

I am running, feet brutally smacking the earth as I tear through the forest. The sound radiates around me, vibrating through the trees and waking the animal kingdom. Birds flock toward the sky, squirrels caw from their nests, and worms slither through the soil. But nothing compares to the hammering in my chest, the steady beats in my mind that cloud my vision.

I never turn around, and I never look back. With each step I take toward freedom, I am equally convinced I am rushing toward certain demise. Around every bend in the path, behind every tree trunk, hidden within each mound of fallen debris, there are rogue vampires. There must be.

By the time I reach the manor, I am still unconvinced it is really there. The alternative is I am already dead, and this is a mirage in the form of an endless nightmare that dangles my deepest desires tauntingly before me. But I refuse to believe death is simply this wicked game of cat and mouse. That would be too cruel a reality regardless of which god or goddess we serve. Perhaps, if I am not dead and if I am not really here, I am dreaming. Maybe my body is still in that cave, and I am trapped within my mind, forever doomed to live out my greatest fears.

But the longer I stare at the Victorian-era home, the more I believe I escaped. I made it. I stared into the eyes of true evil, facing the darkest power I have ever known, and it flinched first. Not only did it fear me, it *released* me. My father was incapable of holding me captive, and now, I intend to stop him.

The feeling of being home, of surviving the day with an army of rogue roommates, is indescribable. Before I found myself a pawn in my father's ruthless game, I didn't appreciate the night or the way it makes the world glisten like magic. I do now, because I shouldn't be here. The truth is, one hybrid against a slew of rogues doesn't equal a favorable survival rate. I should have died tonight. But I didn't, and now the world around me looks anew.

The moonlight cascading down makes the manor look breathtakingly beautiful. With startling overhangs, stained-glass windows, and a weathervane piercing the sky, it is an eerily haunting presence. The gargoyle is perched at the very top stair of the wraparound front porch, and I swear he is smiling at me, like he too welcomes me home.

Slick with dew, the ground sparkles. The cobblestone path from the stairs leads to the wrought-iron fence, which encircles the entire property.

But I am nowhere near it.

I am still submerged within the trees, standing far enough back so I can't be seen by my friends inside. Everything about this place feels like a safe haven, yet I am unable to take that first step forward. It shouldn't be this difficult to emerge from the woods, to announce my presence and beg the hunters for forgiveness. But it is because I don't deserve their love or trust. Not after what happened.

My gaze settles on the gate door—and the missing rod beside it. I blink, and I am back in time, not even twenty-four hours earlier. The entity confined within the crystal controlled my body and nearly killed my friends. I used this now-missing metal pole, tip adorned with two sharp slabs of steel in the form of a cross, to subdue Jeremiah. The worst role in a nefarious game is that of the one incapacitated. The onlooker. The one forced to watch a tragedy unfold, utterly incapable of stopping it. That is what I did to Jeremiah. I wounded him to the point of making him unable to contribute. I wanted him to watch me murder the others—and I almost succeeded. I almost killed my friends.

With a shaky resolve, I take a step forward. By the time I reach the gate, my legs are heavy, and I find it almost impossible to pass the threshold. Feeling lightheaded and anxious, I teeter sideways, feet unsteady, and I grab on to the first thing that will catch my fall. Closing my eyes, I take a deep breath, releasing it slowly as I gather my bearings. Not until I open my eyes do I see what kept me upright.

My hand is clasped around a cross, fingers entwined with metal in a meaty grip. I stare at it for a long time, chest heaving as I process what I am seeing.

Shortly after I became a vampire, we discovered the cross symbol did not burn me. As a hybrid—half witch, half vampire—I was immune to its power against the undead. But when I began to merge with the evil entity summoned by my coven, it scalded my flesh, a bold proclamation proving I was losing my humanity to the darkness. Now that the entity is mute, choosing to slumber ever since I encountered the rogue army, the cross does not harm me.

As I continue to stare at it, unblinking, my vision begins to blur, but I can't help it. I can't look away. I am frozen in time, gaze glued to the startling realization of just how far gone I was. Internally, I wanted to break free. I wanted to destroy the amulet and safely release the magic inside, but the entity was stronger. It overpowered me, silenced me, stole my voice so my friends couldn't hear my silent screams. They had no idea that I was in trouble until it was too late. Luckily, I am the kind of girl who prefers to save herself.

I release the iron stake and walk toward the manor, ascending the steps quickly. I stand before the front door, hand hovering over the knob. Already, I can hear my friends inside. Their voices waft closer, and they are talking about me. With one final huff for courage, I twist the handle and step inside.

It takes five steps from the front entrance to cross the foyer, but it feels like a hundred. The hunters are in the parlor, which is to the right of the entryway. I hide behind the door frame, not bothering to close the front door, and watch them.

The shelves lining the walls are empty, and mounds of books are scattered in heaps on the floor. Holland is among them, with Jeremiah in the chair beside him. Hikari and Malik are sitting on the sofa opposite the others, and Jasik is pacing by the fireplace, arms clenched across his chest. The heat of the flames makes my skin crawl, a sick reminder that I burned only hours ago. If my father hadn't pulled me back into the shadows, charring his own arms in the process, I would be dead right now.

For a long moment, I stare at my sire, wanting so desperately to crawl into those trembling arms. It is true that I assumed the hunters were forever lost to me, and I suppose I deserved the agony that caused, but of them all, I would miss Jasik the most. He has become so much more than just my sire. He is a friend, a lover, a confidant. He is everything I didn't know I needed in this life, and I snapped his neck, nearly taking his head clean off.

I shiver, gaze trailing the room until I find Jeremiah. Sitting on the wingback chair with his legs sprawled in front of him, he is holding a stack of books. One by one, he begins to hand them to Holland, who is positioned on the floor directly beside him. Holland scans the titles and places them in piles that likely resemble order in his mind. It looks like chaos to me.

Jeremiah appears to be fully healed from my attack, but I know that is likely because he drained several dozen blood bags. With enough blood and rest, I knew he would be okay physically, but I am not sure our emotional connection will survive that fight.

"We must find her," Jasik says.

"But where would we look?" Hikari asks. She shifts upright in her seat, resting her elbows on her knees.

"Where would she go if she couldn't come here?" Malik asks.

"Home," Jeremiah says.

I don't miss the sourness in his voice. He is still bitter about what I did, and the fact that he calls my mother's house my *home* tells me we have a long road ahead of us if we want to mend our shattered relationship. Even though it hurts, I don't blame him for being angry with me.

"She wouldn't go there," Jasik says. "Not again."

"How can you be sure?" Malik asks.

"She's gone there several times after being told not to," Hikari points out. "She might go again."

"There isn't anything left of that house," Jasik says plainly. "It's rubble. Besides, *this* is her home now. She knows that."

"Does she?" Hikari asks. "After what happened, I would expect turning to us would be a last resort. I certainly wouldn't come back here if I were her."

"Agreed," Jeremiah says, voice hard.

Jeremiah's eyes are narrowed when he joins the conversation, but when he returns his focus to Holland, who is curled on the floor beside him, he softens. Holland smiles up at him and offers his hand. He squeezes it gently before grabbing a book from the stack Jeremiah is holding. Holland scans the spine and drops the tome onto a pile before grabbing another text.

"She's lived in this town her whole life, right?" Hikari asks. "I'm sure she knows of places where she can hide out until sunset."

"Perhaps she sought refuge with witches," Malik offers. "She may still have friends in this town."

Jasik shakes his head. "She wouldn't. She knows the risks."

"It's also pretty risky to try and kill your friends," Jeremiah says. "But that didn't stop her."

I curse internally. I understand his frustration, and if I were him, I'd hold a grudge too. But that doesn't lessen the sting. I hate that he hates me this much. I fear nothing I say will matter.

"I have to side with Jasik," Holland says. He offers Jeremiah a weak smile before continuing. "The witches in this town know she's a vampire. They won't help her."

"How can you be so sure?" Malik asks. "If she has lived in Darkhaven for seventeen years, she has certainly made friends."

"Mortals befriending immortals just doesn't happen," Holland explains. "Those of us willing to set aside our differences are a rare breed."

"I agree," Hikari says. "You're the only witch I've ever met who hasn't tried to kill us."

"I suppose it is more likely that she is hiding somewhere alone," Malik says, nodding. "She certainly should know of a few vacant buildings where she can rest undisturbed."

"When we last spoke, she said she was looking for someone," Jasik says. "A dreamwalker. She needed to find him to make this right."

"Do you know who the dreamwalker is?" Malik says, eyes on Holland.

He shakes his head. "Astral projection is sometimes referred to as dreamwalking, so I can assume she is referring to a spirit witch. They're the only ones with access to the astral plane. It is the spirit element that grants them entry."

"But we don't know who this spirit witch is?" Hikari asks.

"Spirit witches harness a rare, coveted power," Holland says. "Most elemental control is for a single element—fire, water, earth, or air—but spirit witches can tap into them all. These are rare creatures, but they aren't just in Darkhaven. This dreamwalker could be clear across the planet."

"So just any spirit witch could jump into her mind?" Jasik asks.

"Well, no," Holland says. "This person either has permission to do so or—"

"Permission?" Hikari says.

"Ava's mother was a spirit witch too, which is likely how Ava became a spirit witch," Holland says. "Because of their connection, her mother could enter her dreams whenever she wanted. Kind of like permission."

"So Ava must know this witch personally?" Malik asks.

"Either she knows this witch *or* he is insanely powerful."

"Why do you say that?" Malik asks.

"Because it would take a very strong witch with total control over his spirit power to enter the mind of a hybrid without permission," Holland says.

"Either way, the dreamwalker sounds dangerous," Malik says.

"I think we can assume Ava does not know this witch," Jasik says. "She said she needed to find him, but it was clear she didn't know where he was or even *who* he was. I think she is just as confused as we are."

"What if he is here, in Darkhaven?" Hikari asks. "What if she found him?"

"Then she's in danger," Jasik says.

"Regardless of whether or not she found this witch, she is our responsibility," Malik says. "We need to find her."

"You mean you intend to *stop* her," Jasik says. "What is it you plan to do to her?"

"I will do what I have to do to protect our existence," Malik says. "You should do the same."

"And if she isn't a danger?" Jasik asks. "Will you forgive her, or have you already condemned her to death?"

I hold my breath, waiting for his response. The seconds tick by feeling more like hours. My hands are clammy, my mind is spinning, and I'm shocked my racing heart hasn't alerted them to my presence. Still, I wait in the shadows, unsure if I can handle the truth of his words. I may seek forgiveness, but that doesn't mean I deserve it.

"If she truly wishes to help us destroy the amulet, then I will pardon her mistakes," Malik says. "She can come home, brother. She just has to want to be here."

Jeremiah snorts loudly, rolling his eyes. Holland, who

seems desperate not to get involved, squeezes his lover's knees. This garners Jeremiah's attention but does not soothe his anger. Holland nods at the stack of books he's holding and takes another.

"Jer," Hikari says, voice soft. "We've all made mistakes. We've all done things we regret."

"Maybe you'd feel differently if you were the one nearly staked," he says. His voice is a hiss through his clenched jaw.

"She almost killed us all," Hikari says. "No one left that fight unscathed."

"No one else had to drain a dozen blood bags either," he continues. "I could have died. I think my bitterness is justified."

"Do you intend never to forgive her?" Jasik asks.

"Enough of this," Malik orders. The room silences. "We haven't the time to discuss trivial matters. Yes, you could have died, but you didn't. Right now, that amulet needs to be our sole focus."

"No," Jasik says. "This is an important matter. I need to know if I bring her home, she will be safe here."

"What is the alternative?" Malik asks. "You do not bring her here?"

"Yes. The alternative is we don't come back," Jasik says, utterly emotionless as he stares into the eyes of his only blood relative.

"You would leave?" Hikari asks. "Just like that? Are we not also your family?"

"I have spent plenty of lifetimes in Darkhaven," Jasik says plainly. "If I must relocate, I will."

"No one is leaving," Malik says. He glances at Jeremiah. "And no one is to succumb to petty quarrels. We will discuss her actions, but only after we have destroyed the stone."

"Hello, Ava."

The voice, wicked and vile, is coming from behind me. I know it is her. Every fiber of my body is screaming at me to turn around, but I am frozen, paralyzed in place as I watch my friends continue their conversation as though I am not here.

Each pronounced step of her heel smacking the hardwood floor radiates through the walls around me. It shudders through my arm, which is still resting against the door frame. It shoots down my spine and out the soles of my feet, only to continue the circle again. It repeats, over and over, until the girl halts.

When she stops, she is standing in the doorway, blocking my view. I can no longer see my friends, but what silences my scream is the fact that *they* don't seem to see *her*. They are completely oblivious to our presence.

My gaze flickers between the hunters and the witch. She smiles, likely finding joy in my confusion. I imagine how I look to her, starving and exhausted, as I cling to the shadows, shock strewn across my face. I have never felt as weak as I do in this moment. The air sizzles between us, a haunting reminder of the power hiding within the palm of a fire witch.

"Oh, Ava," Sofia says with a chuckle. "Has it really been that long since you were merely a witch? Has so much time passed, you have forgotten all the fun things magic can do?"

"You spelled them," I whisper.

I already know the answer, so I don't phrase my words as a question. Sofia doesn't treat it as such either. We both know what's happening here. We also know how vulnerable the hunters are, how outmatched I am in my starving state.

"They have no idea you're here," she says confidently, raising her voice to soul-shattering levels.

"But why?" I ask. "I thought you were an ally."

In truth, I never believed she was, but after she risked her neck to protect the vampires, I convinced myself to at least give her a chance. I wanted to believe she could be a friend, even if I only see foe.

The uneasiness is rising in my chest. I push off from the wall and begin walking backward. It takes only seconds to step beyond the doorway threshold, heels teetering over the top porch step. The gargoyle is at my side, but I find no solace in its strength. The books may label it as a protector of vampires, but clearly, that's not the case.

With each backward step I take, Sofía takes two forward. Soon, I am struggling to keep the space between us. Amusement flickers behind her eyes as I clumsily descend the stairs, and her mouth curls into a sly grin.

"How many times have you done this to them?" I ask. "How often do you use magic to influence their decisions?"

"While I do find enjoyment in controlling beings who claim to be all-powerful, I really haven't abused their trust... much," she says. "You would be surprised how much of their actions are their own."

"You're the reason everything is so messed up," I hiss.

She laughs, heartily and loudly, and I wait for the others to come—but they never do. I'm on my own.

"You blame me for the wall between you and your friends, but you built it on your own—brick by brick," she says. "Sure, they make good puppets, but I don't need to master them at all times. You do a wonderful job of it yourself."

"Why are you even here, Sofía?" I ask. "You came for the rogue. I killed him. Why haven't you left yet?"

"Because I quite like it here. I'm not ready to leave, and I know if you had your way, the others would drive me out of town."

"Is that why you are using your magic against them?" I ask, unbelieving. "So you can *stay*?"

It can't possibly be that simple.

Her smile fades, and she shrugs.

"Maybe," she says. "Maybe I'm just tired of being on the road. With the rogue dead, I can finally find a new home."

"And you want to do that *here*?" I ask.

We have walked so far from the front door, I am now passing the wrought-iron fence that surrounds the manor. Even though I know the hunters can't help me should I choose to fight the witch, I still feel agitated that she is forcing the distance between them and me.

"What better place is there than a village like Darkhaven?" she asks. "You have to admit that this town was practically built for the supernatural."

"You're never going to leave, are you?" I ask, voice whisper soft.

I don't bother waiting for a response to a question I already know the answer to. So I retreat. I grant her this victory, knowing she has no intention of harming the others. Like the witches before her, she wants to watch them turn against me, one by one, starting with my sire.

While I make my way to the only person left that I can trust, I think about my father, about the rogue army, and about the murder of my coven. He seems intent on sticking around too. If I am to believe those things are connected, then I cannot dismiss the fact that Sofía arrived at the same time—and she also refuses to leave town.

I have to be smart about this. I am far too weak to face her now. Perhaps if I made better choices in the cave, I wouldn't have used up what little energy I had left. I need to feed, to rest, but most importantly, I need proof. And I need power. I will acquire enough energy to protect my friends and my town from what I fear is the strongest opponent we will ever face—a rogue vampire army controlled by a soulless fiend.

Sofia was right. A dark power is rising in Darkhaven, and it bears the face of my father and the soul of a scorned fire witch.

NINE

The open sign is flashing, but I know it is not welcoming me. Still, I enter Lunar Magic Shop. Immediately, I am assaulted by the wafting fragrance of burning incense. This particular bundle smells like wood and flowers, with a hint of spice. I inhale deeply, ignoring everything else. I close my eyes instinctively, letting the aroma wash over me, and with each breath I take, I feel invigorated, like I am not desperate for blood and sleep. Unfortunately, the slight pep the herbs provide won't last long, so I will need to work quickly.

A girl shrieks, her screams piercing the silent storefront, and I am struck in the chest by something small but heavy. I open my eyes. Luna is standing in front of me, several yards away, and at my feet, there is a white pillar candle. She grabs another from the show table beside her and throws it at me. Unmoving, I watch it soar through the air. It smacks against my stomach and falls to the ground, joining the other.

Perhaps realizing assault-by-candle isn't the best tactic, Luna fumbles with her sweater, shoving her hands deep in its pockets, and she pulls out a small glass jar. She grunts as she opens it—the suction pop vibrating between us—and hurls the contents toward me. Yellow shavings soaked in watered-down juice cascades through the air, and this time, I do move. I take a single step backward, watching as the mixture splatters across the floor. I stare at the mess before returning to her fearful gaze.

Her eyes are wide and ghostly, with red lines laced in the whites and deep divots in her skin. Her long black hair is stringy with oil, and her makeup is smeared. Her arm is still outstretched, hand quivering but intent still threatening, as though her balled fist around a now-empty jar is enough to keep me away. Her mouth is open in a silent scream, and already, she is beginning to sweat. I can smell her fear, but it is punctuated by the pungent odor splashed across my boots.

"Is that..." I trail off, squinting at my toes to confirm my suspicion. I sniff and wince. "Did you just throw a jar of minced garlic at me?"

I am utterly incapable of hiding my shock and amusement. It strains my voice, and I don't know whether to laugh or to scoop a handful and throw it back. Perhaps I will even sample her offering, giving her quite the story to tell later.

Like the first time we met, when I was mesmerized by her beauty and subtle allure, I am now captivated by her mind and her reasoning. Luna is surrounded by ancient texts, most of which are my exact reason for coming here, but she chooses to educate herself by way of films and television shows. Hollywood might claim garlic as a vampire's kryptonite, but really, it is just an overly stinky vegetable.

She shrugs, breathy and exasperated. I see several emotions flash across her face, from embarrassment to delight, but she quickly reverts back to apprehension and doubt. She is suspicious, dreading my true intentions. Luckily, I come in peace.

"It's small and easy to hide," she says slowly.

"Have you been carrying that around all day?" I ask.

"I was afraid you would come back," she says.

"And you thought minced garlic—confined to a glass jar, no less—would stop me?"

I take a step forward, boot smearing the remnants of her weapon into the grain of the hardwood floor.

"Do you realize how much time passed while you struggled to open the jar?" I ask. "If I wanted to hurt you, this wouldn't have stopped me."

I shake my head and exhale dramatically. *Humans.* I don't know how they survive in this world.

"Stop!" Luna shouts as I continue walking forward. "Stay right there! Do not come closer."

I halt and hold up my arms in surrender. I try my best to look nonthreatening, like I didn't try to kill her last night. Coming here wasn't just a last resort—it was my *only* option.

Without access to Holland's occult collection, I am left with only one choice, and as much as I don't want to endanger an innocent or continue to disobey Malik's orders, I need answers. Much to the vampires' dismay, I am willing to risk everything to save us all. They will thank me later.

"You better stay away from me," Luna says, voice shaky but resolve strong.

She adjusts her glasses by pushing them up her nose. They slide down again.

I am impressed by her confidence. Not all humans would do what she is doing after seeing what she has seen. Honestly, most would have left town. I am surprised she didn't.

"Luna..." I begin, but she just frowns and shakes the empty jar at me.

I exhale loudly and run a hand through my matted hair. The girl cringes, nose twitching, and I imagine I smell as awful as I look. I need a shower as desperately as I need a long rest.

"Did you come to kill me?" she asks, voice whisper soft.

I shake my head. "I thought you would have left town. I assumed the store would be vacant."

"Then why are you here?" she asks, narrowing her eyes. She crosses her arms over her chest in defiance.

"I need to look at your inventory," I confess.

"Seriously?" she asks. "You came for a favor? Or did you plan to steal what you need?"

"You have no reason to believe me," I say. "But I promise, I don't want to hurt you. In fact, *I'm sorry*. I really am so sorry for what I did. I wasn't myself last night."

She rolls her eyes and snorts. She takes a single step back, but I remain where I am. I need her to trust me. I need to appear as gentle and placid as possible.

"It has been one day," she says. "One *single* day. I have a hard time believing people are capable of changing at all, so forgive me if I seriously doubt that you had some moral epiphany last night and changed for the better in just a few hours' time."

"Look, you don't have to believe me, but—"

"You need to leave," she says, interrupting me.

"I'm not going anywhere, Luna."

"Well, you're not welcome here," she says plainly.

Her words echo the same sentiment my mother offered me the night I transitioned into a vampire. I hate to admit how much they sting—even now, even coming from a girl I barely know. There is something spectacularly awful about being granted an eternity just to watch everyone around you cut ties.

"I have nowhere else to go," I admit.

"*Shocking*," she says, emphasizing the word. "Maybe you

should be better at making friends. Or maybe you should just stop trying to *kill* people."

She uncrosses her arms, letting them dangle at her sides, and briefly, I note the pity in her eyes. I don't know her well, but I can tell she is a nice person—probably too kind of a soul to be caught up in my drama. But like I said, I am not going anywhere. I need those books.

"Look, I don't have time for this," I say. "I just need to look at your collection. I won't be here long."

She remains quiet for a long time, eyes scanning the length of my short frame. I stay still, a fake smile plastered across my face. I keep my mind busy by picturing myself in her eyes. My pale skin is likely more noticeable now.

Before, she justified my strange behavior and eerie appearance by telling herself lies. This is how humans always react to things they do not understand. They justify what they see by creating a story. They label witches and vampires as overzealous fans of the occult or the supernatural. They imagine us living in dimly lit homes, binge-watching vampire movies all night and sleeping all day. That explains the pale skin, the black attire, the red contact lenses.

But they're wrong, and I think a small part of them knows they're wrong. But they believe the lie nonetheless. Because Hollywood has made humans obsessed with the idea of magic, of raw energy and pure power, of eternal life and limitless energy. This is why Luna turned to garlic as a weapon against me. The media made her do it.

"Are you a vampire?" she asks, finally speaking after the lingering silent minutes between us was becoming almost too much to bear.

I swallow hard, pulse racing. I hoped she wouldn't be

here. I prayed that she left town, abandoning her books and relics. I wished she would never return to Darkhaven. Her disappearance would be one less loose string to sever.

In truth, I have thought about this moment a lot—even before I became the undead. I spent my nights sneaking out of the house to hunt vampires. I spent my days training as the future leader of my coven. My best friend could summon fire with the flick of her wrist, and I had prophetic dreams. It doesn't matter how careful I was; eventually, I would be caught. Someone would see. Either they would witness me controlling the elements or staking a vampire.

This is the time Malik would tell me to lie. To play into the girl's desire for normalcy, for explainable things. I could lie about the night I attacked her. I could even tell her I *wish* I was a vampire—jokingly, of course. We would laugh about our mutual love for paranormal things, and maybe we'd chat about Hollywood's latest attempt at making the creatures we envy.

But I can't lie because *she knows*. She knows what I am, and she isn't running away. She knew I would come for her, and she didn't leave town. Malik would ask me to lie. Jasik would too. But Luna is a human who discovered the existence of magic, and she stayed. I can't deny the importance of that.

So I nod, slowly, and I watch her reaction unfold.

Luna sucks in a sharp breath, and a shiver appears to worm its way through her body. Her skin prickles. I can see the bumps from where I stand. Right now, I imagine her flight instinct is taking over, but she is rooted in place. Her gaze never breaks from mine.

This girl is special.

"My grandmother raised me after my parents were killed," she confesses.

"I, uh, I'm sorry," I say, surprised by her reaction.

"She believed in the old ways."

"The old ways?" I ask, frowning.

I have to admit, this isn't quite how I envisioned the conversation would go, but I appreciate the surprise turn of events. Spontaneity keeps me young.

She nods.

"Before there was religion or science or war, there were the old ways," she says. "She believed in magic, in good and evil, in light versus dark."

"I am not evil." My tone is harder than I intend it to be, and I can't help but wonder who I am trying to convince—her or me.

"But you are born from the blood of a creature that is," Luna says.

"It's not that simple."

"I suppose it isn't," she says. "Most things aren't ever simple, are they? But you did try to kill me last night, so how truthful are you being right now?"

"I wasn't myself," I say, repeating my words from earlier.

"You said that already."

"I also said I'm sorry, and I do mean it. I am sorry."

Luna nods, gaze lowering to the amulet at my chest. I grasp it instinctively, firmly wrapping my fingers around the rough edges of the crystal. The darkness is still silent, but I feel it inside, swirling endlessly within its confines. I wonder what she sees when she looks at it. Does she see the evil inside? Or does she just see stone?

"I won't take your amulet," Luna says.

"You couldn't even if you wanted to," I hiss.

"And you want me to believe that I am safe around you?" she asks.

Slowly, I release the crystal. My arm is heavy, and I feel the pull of the magic as I release it. The darkness doesn't want me to let go, but for now, I am stronger than the entity inside. No longer its puppet, I make my decisions. But for how long? When will the evil regain its strength?

"Do you know what this crystal is?" I ask.

"Of course," she says. "I told you I was raised to believe in the occult. I opened Lunar Magic because I have always felt connected to the spiritual world. I may not be a...vampire, but I certainly know my stones."

"What can you tell me about it?"

"Probably nothing you don't already know," she admits. "You did purchase one of my best texts on crystals."

I nod, letting my mind linger to that tome. It is tucked away at the manor, hidden in my bedroom—the one place I can't go.

"Do you have any more?" I ask.

She frowns and gnaws on her lip. I contemplate remaining silent while she considers my request, because if my promises and apologies haven't been enough, then nothing I say can assure her that she is safe with me. But I haven't the time for this. Too much is at stake.

"Please," I say. "I really need your help."

She sighs heavily, expelling her breath slowly and loudly. She does this again, as though she is working up the courage to agree. I hold my own breath in response because the last thing I want to do is to force her compliance.

What's worse is she and I both know I will if I have to.

"If this is a trick—"

"It's not," I say. "I swear. I just need to do some research, and then—"

She holds up her hand, silencing me. I offer a weak smile.

"If this is a trick, I will spend every minute of my time in the afterlife making you miserable," she says. "I will haunt you every second of every day until you beg for a merciful death, which I will refuse."

She crosses her arms again and points her nose up at me. For the first time in my young life, I think my defiance might be contagious.

I laugh, the heartfelt bellow escaping my lips before I have a chance to take her seriously. I don't stop, even when my stomach hurts. It has been so long since I had a good laugh. It has been too long since I spoke to someone who isn't privy to war or fallen comrades. Luna fears for her life without realizing how much I need her, need *this*. Normality. Simplicity. *Peace*.

"I don't think death works that way," I say, still chuckling. "I mean, I have never met a ghost. Have you?"

"Trust me," she says. "I will have nothing but endless time. I will find a way."

I nod. "Well, I do know something about endless time."

She takes one small step forward, closing the space between us. I don't move, ever fearful she will change her mind. But the closer she comes, the more I wonder if I can do this, if I can overcome my instincts. After all, how does a predator coexist with prey?

TEN

Books are stacked in piles, encircling me in a wall of cracked leather and yellowed pages. I have been here for hours, reading publications that haven't brought me any closer to the knowledge I seek.

I suppose the desire to find answers in these texts was a fool's mission. There are so many things I don't know that won't be written in some random tome, like the truth about Sofía and what happened to my coven, or what my father's plan is for the rogue army and what he will do to this town if I continue to refuse his request to join him.

What I need to solve those mysteries is something I already have—*time*—but I have never been a patient person. If I can force a hand, I will.

Luna has spent the last few hours watching me from afar, rarely venturing close. She has scoured her stock room and inventory lists, searching for anything that might help me answer my questions.

Part of her inability to find me a proper text is her lack of understanding. I haven't divulged any truths. I might have admitted to being a vampire, but I have confessed nothing else. I haven't mentioned the amulet or darkness confined within. I haven't explained the differences between hunters and rogues. I haven't even mentioned the existence of witches and magic.

She may be a believer, but she might not be an ally. I need to tread carefully if I am to win back the hunters' trust.

The shopkeeper approaches swiftly, each smack of her shoes against the hardwood sending shockwaves through my bottom. I am sitting cross-legged on the floor, still surrounded by books with no real progress made. I glance up when she hovers beside me. Her smile is bright and wide, her lips stretching nearly ear to ear like a Cheshire cat.

"Did you find something?" I ask, already knowing the answer. Her eerie appearance makes it quite obvious.

She is holding a book to her chest. The dark-brown leather is cracked by age, the spine creased and thick. The pages are dry and tea stained. They do not lie flat, and the girl struggles to hold the weight of the tome in her feeble arms.

She lets it slide forward, spinning it around until the title—in the form of a striking pressed overlay—blares back at me. Above the title, a symbol is etched in the leather. It is the form of the cross but with a teardrop-shaped loop in place of an upper bar. Save for the title and the ankh symbol, the cover is blank. There is no author byline.

"I think this might have the answers you're looking for," she says.

VAMPYR

Eyes glued to the bold font, I do not speak. Unmoving, frozen in time and place, I simply stare at the book. Luna crouches beside me and places the text in my lap. She is close enough for her long tresses to brush against my arm. The sensation is overpowering, silencing the strong beats of my heart that echo in my mind.

Still, I ignore the desire to reach for her, to entangle my fingers with her hair, because something about this tome calls to me. It speaks like whispers in the wind, a sound that ruffles the leaves and sends shivers down spines. I hear it even now, the wispy confession of a voice I have never before heard. The singsong presence is soft and sweet, and it swirls around me, quelled only when I place a palm to the cover. The voice is muted now, but I still feel its secrets as soft vibrations against my hand.

I lick my lips as I open to the first page. The spine cracks, and the scent of aged paper wafts closer. I inhale deeper, letting it wash over me. It is musty, smelling of ink and wood, smoke and vanilla. The aroma is so strong I can no longer sense the burning incense. I can no longer hear Luna's lungs sucking air or her heart pumping blood through her body. This book, weighty and decrepit, stills my senses.

VAMPYR

"Where did you get this?" I ask hesitantly.

I rub my fingertips across the title page. The texture is rough and makes my hand tingle. I trace designs with my thumb, pressing my finger against the grain of paper. When I look closely, I can see the threaded design; it is woven like magic.

"This is an occult shop," Luna says with a chuckle. "If I come across relics as old as this, especially books with a title like that, I add them to my inventory. I would do my store a great disservice if I passed on the opportunity."

"You hoped to sell this?" I ask. "I imagine it would be difficult to find a buyer."

She exhales loudly and thinks about her answer before speaking.

"Honestly, I assumed it would never sell," she says. "I knew if it ever sold, it would be to a buyer who was looking for this specific text. This isn't the kind of book someone strolling off the street asks about. But it was too beautiful not to buy for the store."

"It might never sell," I say.

"I'm okay with that," Luna says. "I will just add it to my personal collection."

"Have you read it?"

She shakes her head.

"It's not in English," she admits. "Well, a few parts have been translated, albeit poorly so. I tried to read it, but I didn't get past the first page. I mainly just skimmed cover to cover."

I turn the page to scan the contents page, and as I do, the energy pouring from this tome begins to hum. My hands are warming at the sensation, and sweat beads at my temple. The air in the room is shifting, but Luna appears unaffected. She has no idea just how special this book is.

It reacts to me the way a grimoire would to a witch, but this isn't merely some random book of shadows. This text, scrawled in a language likely spoken by very few, contains more than spells and secrets passed down through the family. I don't need to understand its meaning to be sure of that.

"Maybe there is a translated version available somewhere," I say, but even I doubt my words.

"Even if there is, without an author name, I would have no way to find it," she says.

The text inside is handwritten, legible and clear, in the form of symbols, but in a language I have never seen. I flip through the pages with my thumb, stopping when I find notes written in the margins. Like Luna said, not everything has been translated in English, but quite a lot has been translated into Latin—and I happen to speak Latin.

Silently, I thank my mother for the lessons she insisted I take, the very ones I naïvely assumed would do me no good.

I read each page that has been translated. Similarly to what the witches taught me, the author places all vampires into one group—simply noted as *the undead* or just *vampyr*—when he or she should have separated rogues from the others. There are vampires and there are hunters and there are rogues—all of which are different. Why is this so hard for mortals to comprehend?

But the more I read, the more I realize the writer *is* speaking about just *one* vampire. The rogue. The evil, soulless undead. They fear the rogue vampire and urge its annihilation. I can't say I blame them.

The author believes in the existence of vampires and mentions a magical elixir and spellbinding incantation that can protect the living from the dead. But the more I read, the less I find. Too much is left untouched, untranslated.

Still, the pages are not blank. The translator begins to fill the empty space with scribbles in the form of the ankh, scratching the symbol onto the paper hundreds of times. With each page I turn, there seems to be more and more symbols traced, until there is no blank space remaining.

According to what has been translated, the author claims a crystal charged by an elixir can kill a rogue vampire. Much like how medicinal practices evolve over time, tactics to kill vampires must too. If I were still mortal and embarking on my usual patrol, I would prefer fire magic over some witchy concoction that likely will not work.

Though the incantation itself has not been translated, the ingredients are listed in English.

To form the elixir, it notes specific herbs and pink Himalayan salt soaked in water that has been charged by both the sun and moon.

To enchant the stone, it says to charge it by bathing it in the elixir on the night of the full moon. The stone recommended as most powerful for destroying rogue vampires is onyx.

The black onyx crystal.

I gasp, staring at the untranslated sections of perfectly scribbled symbols. The firm strikes and bellowing curves of each shape mock my internal plea for the loops and lines to unravel and translate themselves. Of course, they do not. The book remains in a language unspoken, the knowledge within likely lost to us all.

When I close the text, I think about the amulet I protect, the mute darkness within, and my father. Something about this tome, the way it hums and speaks to me even when I sit in silence, makes me uneasy, uncertain of his true intentions. The author is certainly speaking about rogue vampires, for there are no others deemed vile or nefarious by nature. Rogue vampires are the only true soulless among the undead.

When I think about my father, I am suspicious of his involvement in the murder of my coven. Back at the cave, when I mentioned my mother, long before I admitted her demise, his utter disinterest in seeing her again made me believe he knew she was already dead.

Then I saw her, and she told me she believes the man she loved is dead, and Papá—or whoever this man is—has given me no reason to doubt her. If anything, he has proven her claims by asking me to kill the child, to ignore the innocent, to experience life as a vampire by turning into a monster. He wants me to join him, to rise under his dark power and force this world to its knees. He is like the plague, and he will wash over this land as a river of blood.

A callous beast who shares both my father's face and our memories together is a dangerous creature.

When I stand with the book, my arms feel weak beneath its weight. I reach the register and set down the tome, only to feel the immediate pull of it now that it is no longer shielded by my arms. It hums, silently begging to be cradled once again.

Luna, seemingly oblivious, taps a few buttons on her register and announces the total.

Only then do I realize I have no money. What little funds I did have was spent on the last book I bought at this store. Ever since I transitioned, the last thing on my mind has been finances.

I stare at the shopkeeper, unable to admit that I can't afford the book—but I can't leave without it either.

"You can just take it," she says courtesy of her newfound ability to read my mind, or maybe the look of dread creasing my face in horror gave me away.

"I can't do that," I say, even though every fiber of my body wants to grab it and run. I mean, stealing something is better than killing for it, right?

"Let's be honest," she says lightheartedly. "It's better off with you than me."

She's right. It is.

I exhale slowly as I glance down at the book, swallowing the knot that forms in my throat. Yesterday, I tried to kill this girl. And today, she just might be saving my life. This book has answers—I can *feel* it. Its translations note rogue vampires and the black onyx crystal, but perhaps Holland and I can uncover more, like how to destroy the dark entity for good.

"I promise," I say. "I will pay you back."

I exit the magic shop and halt.

A woman is standing before me, her frame illuminated by a nearby streetlight. She is tall and thin, with striking curls that are wild and frizzy. Her hair blows softly in the night air, and she is smiling at me, soft but sincere.

"Hello, Ava," she says, voice deep and husky.

I know this woman. I recognize her as a witch from another coven. She was friends with my mother, though I don't know her name.

Still, I am drawn to her. Not because she is a familiar face or because she befriended Mamá. But because she stood on the front porch of a burned down house now in rubble with a bouquet of flowers in her arms and tears streaking her red, puffy cheeks. She was there to mourn when no one else was.

She takes a step forward, and I step back.

"You do not need to fear me, girl," she says.

"You're a witch," I say.

"As you once were," she says. "Or have you forgotten your past so quickly? Eternity is a long time to lose one's memory."

"What do you want?"

She glances at my amulet, gaze lingering too long for my liking. I fight the urge to shield it, but when it drops to the book in my hand, I tense. I suck in a sharp breath and force myself to calm down. Internally, I remind myself that I am the strong one. I am the vampire. She is a witch. I may be exhausted and starving, but I can certainly handle *one* witch. Right?

My mind flashes to Sofía—and to the vampires I left alone with her—and I am ashamed that I granted one witch so much power over me. I have decided I will confront Sofía—as long as I make it home.

"I came to warn you," she says.

I frown, preparing myself for what is likely a weak threat. She is going to tell me that she will kill me if she ever finds me in Darkhaven again, and I am going to tell her it will take more than a witch to scare me away.

"The humans are becoming suspicious," she says. "They have brought in outsiders to investigate that fire."

I swallow hard, shaking my head, surprised by the direction this conversation has taken. I was prepared to defend my need to be here, to stay in the only town I have ever known. But I was not prepared to become the sole suspect in my mother's murder. This witch might hate me for what I am, but she can't possibly believe I caused the death of my family, of my coven.

"I—I have nothing to do with that," I say. "I wasn't even there."

"I know," she says. "You haven't lived there for months."

"Then why would—"

"You must leave, Ava," she says, interrupting me. "Leave Darkhaven and never return."

I am stunned silent save for the breath escaping my gaping mouth. I scoff at her suggestion, as if I could ever actually leave. Darkhaven is my home. I lost *everything* in my pursuit to save this town, and I will not abandon it now.

"It isn't safe for you here," she explains. "It isn't safe for any of us."

ELEVEN

Day is beginning to break, and the sky is growing brighter with every passing second. The moon is still glowing overhead, the stars still twinkling beyond it, but the sun is rising over the horizon, a looming threat, a fateful promise.

I spent all night at the magic store, and much to my surprise, Luna never asked me to leave, even when the minutes ticked by like nagging murmurs, a constant reminder that all is not well. The hours have settled over us now—for her, like a thick, comfortable blanket; for me, like a noose.

My breath catches in my throat as I cross the threshold, taking a single step into the foyer. I close the door behind me, the crashing sound echoing through the silent passageway. This time, they hear me.

The hunters approach swiftly, but my gaze settles on Jasik. He rushes over, pulling my body against his. He wraps his arms around me, fingers digging into the flesh at my spine. I wince at the pressure, but I welcome the pain. I was expecting a far worse outcome.

I am still holding the book Luna gave me, but Jasik has cocooned me in his embrace. My hands rest against his chest, the edge of the tome jabbing into his torso. He doesn't move, doesn't release me. He simply holds on tightly, as if I might slip free.

I exhale slowly, deeply, releasing the tension that has built up over the last twenty-four hours. Standing on my tiptoes, I lean against him, and he supports my weight as I nuzzle into the curve of his neck. I breathe him in. He smells like blood and peppermint. I take another gulp of his musk, letting it wash over me.

"I thought..." my sire whispers, breath fluttering my hair. The words he chooses not to say linger in the air.

He thought I was dead. He thought I would never come home. He thought I might have completely merged with the darkness, my soul forever lost to its depths.

"I'm okay," I say, but my assurance falls flat.

He pulls away, holding me back so he can assess the damage done. His hands clasp around my arms, and his eyes scan the length of my body. This is the moment he takes it all in—from my singed clothes, to my matted hair, to my dirty fingernails, to my bloodstained skin. I am covered in soot, and I reek. The odor permeating through the hall is thick, and Jasik scrunches his nose when he takes a deep breath.

"Are you hungry?" he asks.

I smile at him, eyes swelling from emotion. The last thing on his mind is my betrayal. He cares more about my wellbeing than my whereabouts. I'm sure the others are far less concerned with my appetite, so I don't dare look at them.

"I'm starving," I say, voice shaky.

"Come," he says. "You need to feed."

Together, with Jasik's arm wrapped protectively around my shoulders, we walk through the manor, bypassing the others. The farther the walk, the more I fear meeting their gazes. I dread what I will see.

My sire might forgive me, but will they? Malik might

have sworn leniency if I returned a willing participant in their desperate charade to destroy the amulet, but now that I am here, does he still want that? Does he still want me to be a member of this nest?

In the kitchen, I sit and carefully place the book on the table beside me. I rest my elbows on either side and cradle my head against my palms. I close my eyes and breathe slowly. The steady thumping in my head has intensified. It is so loud now, I can barely hear Jasik prepare my meal.

"I don't know why I feel so awful," I admit.

"You need to feed," Jasik explains.

"It has only been one night."

"Vampires may bear the mark of immortality, but we can die like any other creature," Jasik says. "We need rest and blood to survive. Like humans, the more energy we deplete, the weaker we become."

I sit back, running a hand through my hair. My fingers tangle in the knotted tresses, so I free them and leave the snarled mound at the crown of my head.

Jasik walks over and hands me a mug of nuked blood.

I gulp it greedily, closing my eyes to inhale the aroma. The coppery scent of blood is tinged by sweetness. It smells like ripe fruit and wilting flowers, like life *and* death, all at the same time.

By the time my belly is full, several blood bags have been drained, and I am finally starting to feel a little better, the pounding in my head becoming nothing more than a soft knock. I still need rest, but now that my mind is clearing, I can face the others.

I open my eyes to find Jasik sitting at the table in the seat across from me, and even though we are alone in the room, I sense the presence of others. The hunters are just outside the door, eavesdropping. I don't blame them. I wouldn't trust me either.

"Tell me what happened," Jasik says.

"I have been seeing a man in my dreams," I begin. "A spirit witch."

"You left to find him?" Jasik asks.

I nod. "I thought he might be able to help us."

"Why would a stranger help us?"

"Every time he entered my dreams, he warned me about the amulet," I say. "He wanted me to destroy the stone before it was too late."

"So you thought he might know how to do that?"

"I hoped so," I say. "I knew it was a long shot, but after what happened last night, I had no other choice."

"Did you find him?" Jasik asks.

I shake my head. "I found . . . I found someone else."

Jasik frowns, brow furrowing.

"I stumbled on a cave system, deep in the forest. There were . . . *hundreds* of rogue vampires living there. An army. An army of rogues."

Jasik freezes, jaw agape, stunned silent. I am not surprised by his shock, but I still feared it. His reaction tells me this is abnormal—and not a lot of things are new to a vampire who has lived a thousand lives.

The door to the kitchen swooshes open, and the hunters file inside. One by one, I am surrounded. We forgo pleasantries.

"Are you sure?" Malik asks. "Are you absolutely positive there were that many rogue vampires in one nest?"

"Rogues tend to be solitary creatures," Hikari adds. "They live alone or in very small nests."

"I'm positive," I say.

"Did you fight them?" Jasik asks. He glances down, gaze lingering on my bloody clothes. "Is that why you are so weak?"

I wrap my arms around my chest, scratching at the exposed skin on my arm where the sleeve of my jacket ripped. I still haven't seen myself in a mirror, but I can imagine how awful I look.

"Tell us everything," Malik says.

"By the time I found their nest, it was too late to turn back," I say. "The sun was rising, and I wouldn't have time to make it all the way home. I tried to stay to the shadows, to keep quiet. I thought I could camp for the day and leave at dusk. I thought they might never know I was even there."

"But they found you," Jasik says, voice soft and steady.

I nod. I glance at Jeremiah, whose gaze is hard, emotionless. I squeeze my eyes shut, but the images of his anger, his distrust remain.

"How did you face that many rogues and survive?" Hikari asks.

"There was a boy," I whisper, voice cracking. "They were going to kill him."

I open my eyes, and with tears streaming down my cheeks, I decide to tell them everything.

"It was worth it," I begin. "Everything I did was worth it because it led me there. It led me to him, and I *saved* him."

"Did you kill them?" Malik asks.

"Some, but the rest remain."

"Why didn't you just use the amulet?" Jeremiah asks. "You had no trouble using it against us."

Jasik clears his throat, the sound loud and harsh in the silence of the room. He shoots Jeremiah an angry glare before his gaze settles back to me, eyes softening.

"I tried," I admit. "I was convinced my only escape would be to use the amulet to kill them all at once, but it didn't work."

"What do you mean it didn't work?" Holland says.

The witch is standing beside Jeremiah, fingers entwined with his lover's hand. He remains a steady source of strength for the weak vampire.

"I tried to summon the magic, but I couldn't."

"Maybe it broke," Hikari says, hopeful. "Maybe it's *over*."

Holland shakes his head. "Magic doesn't work that way. Amulets don't just stop working."

"I feel the entity inside," I say. "It's still there. It's just choosing to remain silent."

"Good," Jeremiah says.

"How did you escape without using the amulet?" Malik asks.

"Your clothes are singed," Jasik says. He reaches forward, fingertips brushing against the burned threads of my jacket.

"I had to do it," I say. "To save him, to save the boy, I had to do it. There wasn't another way."

"What did you do?" Jasik asks slowly, voice heavy with dread. He already knows. They all do, I'm sure.

"I grabbed him, and I ran," I say. "I knew I couldn't face them all on my own, and I knew they couldn't follow me outside. Not while the sun was out."

Hikari gasps. Her gaze lingers on my appearance, and I think I see the exact moment the dots connect for her.

"The heat of the sun was like nothing I have ever experienced," I say. "It was fiercer than any magical hex I have endured at the hands of the witches. But the boy survived. I would do it again if I had to."

"You could have died," Malik says. "You *should* have died, but I am glad you're okay. It is important you know that."

"How are you still here?" Hikari asks. "How did you survive that?"

"A rogue pulled me back inside," I say. "But the boy already started running, so even though he dragged me back into that cave, he was too late to catch the child."

"You're lucky," Hikari says. "I don't know anyone who has survived both direct sunlight *and* the number of rogue vampires you say reside in that cave."

"Is there anything else you can tell us?" Malik asks. "Rogue nests, in general, are quite uncommon, so a nest of this size is unheard of. Anything at all you can remember will be helpful."

"They have a leader," I say slowly. "He controls them. He tells them what to do, and they listen. They obey. I thought... I thought that was impossible."

"It is," Malik says. "At least, it should be. Rogues are controlled by their blood lust, having little restraint for anything else."

"We must kill him," Hikari says. "We can take no chances."

Malik nods. "One rogue with that much self-control and innate power is too great a threat."

"Is there anything you can tell us about him?" Jasik asks. "His name, his appearance, anything at all that might help?"

I swallow hard before speaking, mentally preparing myself to condemn my father to death.

"I know his name," I say slowly. "It's my father. The rogue vampire is my father."

The room is silent. The steady ticks of the clock hanging on the wall are all I hear. The hunters look at each other, likely telepathically communicating how to proceed without causing me to have an emotional breakdown. Luckily for them, I am too exhausted for another one. I'm at my lowest point, so there is nowhere to go but up.

My sire is the first to speak.

"Your ... father?" Jasik asks. "He's alive? Your father is alive, and he's the rogue vampire controlling the army?"

"My father is a rogue vampire," I say, still unbelieving.

"Did he come back for you?" Jasik asks.

I nod. "He says he did."

"How convenient," Hikari says with a snort. "I think we can all admit the timing is suspicious."

"I must agree with Hikari," Malik says. "Why now? After all these years, why come back now? The only thing that has changed is you, Ava. You are no longer the witch he left. You are a vampire hybrid."

"Did you ask him about the fire?" Hikari asks. "He probably lit the match himself."

"Let's not jump to conclusions," Malik says. "Although, it does seem likely he is privy to information we need about that fire."

"I think ..." I sigh heavily. "I think he killed them. I think he killed my mother as a way to get to me."

"He's dangerous, Ava," Jasik says. "We need to stop him."

I sniffle, fingers swirling around the edge of my mug. I process his confession, knowing the words are true to my heart. I am unconvinced this vampire is even my father, but he looks like Papá. He *feels* like Papá, and that alone makes it difficult for me to turn my back on him.

"I know," I say, voice breaking.

"Ava, this man is not your father," Malik says. "Your father died the moment he turned rogue."

"He's right," Jasik says. "He might look like your father. He might sound like the man you remember. But it's not him. Not anymore."

"How can you be sure?" I ask.

"Vampires and rogues are different," Malik says. "The vampire got his body, but he didn't get his soul. That's gone. That was released the moment he aligned with darkness."

"He's a monster," I say, mirroring Malik's words.

"Rogues are particularly malicious creatures," Malik confirms. "They are soulless and vile, living simply for the kill. They care about little else than sating their blood lust. This is why a rogue vampire with the mental capability to lead others is so dangerous."

"Jasik is right," Holland says. "He absolutely must be stopped."

"I have a question that no one wants to hear," Hikari says. "How do we know he isn't a *hybrid* rogue vampire? He was a witch, like Ava. He became a vampire... like Ava."

"I suppose that might explain why he is unlike the others," Malik says.

"He never used magic at the cave," I say. "But I didn't either. I didn't want him to know, just in case."

"That was smart," Malik says. "But he says he came back for you, so there is little chance he is unaware that you are a hybrid."

I glance at the others, gaze lingering from vampire to vampire. Jeremiah's icy stare is warming... I think. I hope. I smile at him, and he doesn't look quite as disgusted as he did the moment I came home. Maybe he pities me, knowing I will bury both parents in the course of just a few days.

I don't want his pity. I want his friendship.

"I know I don't deserve your trust or your forgiveness," I say. "But I want you all to know how sorry I am. I never meant to hurt anyone, least of all you guys."

Jasik reaches for me, clasping his hands over mine. I don't need to look at him to know he has forgiven me. His love for me knows no bounds and can be hindered by nothing I do. I don't deserve him. I don't deserve any of them.

"We know that you weren't yourself," my sire says. "But you must understand how dangerous that amulet is."

"I want to be clear," Malik says. "We will allow you back as long as you help us destroy the stone."

"I will," I say. "I promise."

TWELVE

I swipe the steam from the mirror, a solid slash across the glass, and stare at my blurred reflection. I don't look the same. My eyes are sunken, with deep crevices beneath each socket. My skin is taut and pale, my frame thin and bony. I look more like a living skeleton than a daughter of the night.

Before my eyes, my body begins to rejuvenate as the blood I drank works its way through my system. The process is agonizingly slow, but it captivates me nonetheless. I watch as my lifeless eyes begin to glimmer, as my skin begins to plump, as weakness turns to strength. By morning, I'll look completely different. I'll look like me again.

Feeding and cleansing might have washed away the raw truth of my time in that cave—the blood and soot, the dirt and decay, the starvation and deprivation—but everything else remains. The mental duress, the emotional exhaustion is all-consuming now that I am free.

When I exit the bathroom, I find Jasik waiting on my bed. He is sitting with his elbows resting on his thighs, and he stares at the floor. I don't need to be psychic to know he is worried about me, about us. He fears for my safety, for the longevity of this nest. He is concerned about the amulet and the entity within.

But the darkness is silent now. It swirls within the stone,

confined to an eternity of nothingness. Before today, it wasn't okay with such a fate, but something changed.

"How are you feeling?" Jasik asks without looking up.

"Better," I say. "Tired."

He nods. "You need rest."

"Are you angry with me?"

He glances up, finally meeting my gaze, and he smiles softly. It is small and weak, but the sincerity of it reaches his eyes, and my heart explodes. The tension melts away, and it is a little bit easier to breathe, to think, to live. The worst part about what happened wasn't losing myself to the darkness. It was disappointing those I love.

"I could never be angry with you," he says.

I sit beside him on the bed. Our fingers entangle, threading together like perfect puzzle pieces, and he squeezes my hand three times. He has done this before, and each time he does it, I feel his love for me.

"I feel ... strange," I admit. "Like I'm forgetting something important."

"You will feel better tomorrow," he assures me.

I swirl my thumb in circles, tracing invisible shapes across his skin. He shivers at the sensation, and I feel my own prickle in response. My body reacts to his—to his nearness, to his scent, to his affection. The invisible string that pulls us together coils tightly, and I feel myself drawn closer, eliminating the space that separates us.

"You know I'm sorry, right?" I ask.

Fearing his reaction, I don't look at him when I say this, but he surprises me by reaching over. With his index finger beneath my chin and thumb nestled firmly against the divot, he lifts my gaze to meet his.

"You know I love you, right?" he says, mimicking my expression.

His tone is playful, joyfully mocking, but I don't doubt his words for even a moment.

There is something between us. It has always been there, from the moment we first met on the night of that fateful full moon ritual. Since childhood, I have heard stories of a love so grand it is etched in stone, marked for eternity as not just a thing of beauty but as the proclamation of true destiny. *Fate*. Now, when I think of that love, I think about *him*. We were meant to meet, to find each other, even though we were born to different worlds. Thankfully, true love knows no bounds.

A vampire and a witch. It's not supposed to be a love connection, yet here we are.

I press my lips to his, unlocking our hands so I can slide my fingers through his tresses. He moans, the bellow vibrating from deep beneath his sternum. His kiss is intense and consuming, longing and needy.

Body humming, I straddle his lap, and we fall back together, landing in a mound of sheets.

When we finally pull away, we are breathless, bodies entangled, my head against his chest, the steady beats of his overworked heart lulling me to sleep.

For a moment, I allow myself this happiness, this peace, convincing my tired mind that the terror encroaching Darkhaven is only a nightmare.

I am surrounded by a fine mist, particles in the air swirling round and round like a snow globe, and even though I should be concerned about my whereabouts, I am still haunted by the realization that I have forgotten something urgent. It eats away at my innards, and having feasted on my body as I slept, it has made me nothing but goo.

But I can't worry about that now, because I am dreaming.

I am standing in my bedroom—the one I lost to flame and fury. I am hovering beside the bed where I used to sleep, but it is vacant now.

The longer I stare at this empty room, shattered and dank, the foggier the air becomes. The intensity is suffocating, so I stand in silence, watching, waiting, somehow knowing what is coming. But like last time, I won't be able to stop it. I can't save what is already gone.

My legs are heavy, my steps deliberate, but I finally reach the door. The handle is hot, and it burns my palm. But I open it anyway.

The heat is nauseating, igniting a rush of bile that scalds the back of my throat. I wash it down with spit and disgust as I continue navigating through the house by way of memory.

The smoke is thick and strong, blinding me, but I know these halls, these stairs, these rooms. Of course, they are all gone now. The wood used to build our sanctuary has succumbed to the force of a greater threat—fire.

I descend the steps and enter the foyer. That hall leads me deeper into the belly of the house. I blink, and I am staring at the door that leads to the basement. It is firmly closed, the knob glowing bright red. I touch it, and my skin sizzles. I linger too long, and the scent of seared flesh makes my stomach rumble.

I open the door and am greeted by darkness. The billowing smoke tickles my lungs, and I hack. The sensation is too much, but I can't turn away. Not now. Not when I know they are down there.

Slowly, I take each step, the wood creaking under my weight. I reach the basement floor and sink into the soft dirt. No longer compact and solid, it too wishes to escape a fiery demise.

I am not alone.

The witches are here, on bended knees, begging for their lives. They do not see me because I am not really here. This is just a dream. A nightmare. An opportunity to torture myself by remembering how I failed them.

But he is here. His back is to me. The witches plead with him, hands clasped in prayer as they ask my father for mercy.

The light dances across his silhouette, playing tricks on my weakened mind. I blink, and I am suddenly closer to him, but I am certain I have not moved. He does not turn to greet me, does not even know I am here, watching, waiting, witnessing the horrific act he committed.

I know what happens next, and I don't want to see it.

There is a match in his hand, and it is lit. The flame burns through the wood stick, slowly sinking toward his fingers. It won't be long now. The end is almost here.

But Mamá looks at me, tears streaming down her cheeks. She stares into the darkness, and I am certain she sees me— *really* sees me. Her eyes glimmer with hope, and she tricks herself into believing I am a savior. But I am no hero. I am the reason they died weak and powerless, utterly incapable of defending themselves.

"Please," she whispers, voice strained and murky.

I think she is speaking to me. The pain in her voice pierces my heart, and right then, I decide I will save them. Every night in my dreams, I will save them.

He is close enough to touch, so I reach for him, but the pull of my weighty arm is slow. By the time my hand brushes against his back, fingers scrunching his jacket in a vise-like grip, the match has almost ignited his skin.

He turns at the same time I pull him to face me, but as he moves, his body morphs from that of my father to someone I know all too well.

Jasik stares back at me.

I am stunned silent, jaw agape as I look into the soulless eyes of my lover. They are blood red and hollow. He bears fangs, and he laughs. He *laughs* as he flicks the match toward the witches, and they are lit aflame.

In the glow of the flickering light, I see his face, marked by shadows, and he is smiling at me.

When I open my eyes, I stare at the ceiling for a long time. Fear has made my heart swell, and the urgency to rise, to find my sire, is overwhelming. But I remain still, counting each swoosh of the overhead fan and focusing on my breath to slow my racing heart.

"It was just a nightmare," I whisper. "It wasn't real."

But even though I am sure my overactive imagination is to blame, I cannot release the anxiety plaguing me. It has gripped my chest, squeezing until my organs pop and gush.

I hold up my hand and stare at my untouched palm. I can still feel the heat of the flame, the fire that licked my skin as it burned my family alive. I can still see his smile and the malice that resided there.

I glance over. The spot where Jasik sleeps is vacant, the

sheets unruffled and cool. The bathroom door is closed. I wait for him to return to me, but he never shows. The silence coming from the other room is louder than I can bear.

"Jasik?" I say, voice cracking.

He does not respond.

I stand, and when I reach the bathroom door, my hand hovers over the knob, frozen in fear. I say his name again as I tap lightly on the wood with my index finger, but only the quiet is listening.

I yank the door open. The room is dark, empty. I am alone. Jasik is gone.

I spin on my heels. The bedroom has not changed. Save for the blankets bunched in a bundle at the foot of the bed, where I tossed them aside, everything is where I left it.

Except for him. Except for Jasik.

All at once, I remember what was forgotten.

"*Sofía*," I hiss.

THIRTEEN

It takes less than thirty seconds for me to search the house for Jasik. He is nowhere to be found.

I stand silently in the sitting room, staring at the stairwell that leads to the second floor. The hunters are still slumbering, still waiting for the sun to set. They have no idea that their brother is missing, that the very witch likely responsible is in their midst.

With fists balled at my sides, my body begins to tremble. I breathe loudly through my nose, and for a long time, the sucking noise of air entering and exiting my lungs is all I can hear. I am desperate to calm the tremors, to convince myself that I am overreacting, but I fail miserably at subduing the anger and dread that overwhelm me.

The more I think about Sofía, the more I remember. It is all coming back to me now—the moments I forgot, the things I wanted to say. I planned to confront her, but magically, I didn't. I crossed the threshold, entering the manor, and my memory failed me.

There isn't a speckle of doubt in my mind that the witch knows something. She knows why I conveniently lost my memory, and she knows what happened to my sire. She did this to me, to him. And she will pay.

The footsteps of someone approaching echo all around

me. My gaze trails the steps, lingering on the top landing. I see his feet first. He wears socks, no shoes. As he descends, he is in full view. Still wearing sweatpants but no T-shirt, Malik yawns loudly, dramatically as he emerges. He halts when he sees me.

"Ava?" he says, voice groggy. He squeezes his eyes shut and opens them again, like I might be a mirage. "What's wrong? Are you... Are you okay?"

He walks toward me, steps hesitant, and he reaches my side before I even speak. He touches my arm, fingertips grazing my skin. The sensation makes me shiver.

I meet his eyes and stare into their crimson depths. He looks so much like his brother. For a moment, I wonder what it would be like to look at Malik, seeing Jasik in his eyes, knowing I will never again feel the comfort of my lover's arms.

"What happened?" Malik asks.

Panic stricken, with pictures of Jasik, weak and desperate, flickering behind my eyes, I still don't respond. I distract myself by focusing on the sound of the others approaching.

I hear Jeremiah's voice, loud and deep. Holland responds, giggling feverishly. Hikari is there. She snorts, and I imagine her eyes rolling. She is a sucker for love, even though she tries hard to convince us otherwise.

"Where is Jasik?" Malik asks.

His hand grips my arm and squeezes gently, as if to ground me in this moment. He knows I am losing myself, my mind responding to all the little noises around us—none of which belong to *him*.

"Jasik..." I whisper, saying his name, and somehow, I think Malik knows. I don't have to tell him. He doesn't need to force the words from my breaking heart. He. Knows. Just like I know.

He's gone.

No longer in this house, he was taken. Intruders emerged by way of night, cloaked in shadows, stealing the only thing I have to live for anymore.

Everything moves slowly. I blink, the movement painstakingly raw and heavy, like my swollen heart. I turn, craning my neck to look at the others. They are silent now, each watching my exchange with Malik. And I see it. The exact moment they know too. Something is wrong. Jasik is missing.

I see her as she emerges from behind the group. The gasp, the sound crackling and rough. My breath catches in my throat as we lock gazes, and she smiles. She *smiles*.

I am in front of her before she has a chance to react, before she even realizes how quickly I can end her life. It's already over. She just doesn't know it yet.

My hand is at her throat, and yielding to a superior strength, her body is soaring through the air, until it crashes against the wall. She remains in my grasp, and I tighten my grip on her flesh.

She screams and claws at my hands, desperate to free herself, but I have her pinned in place. She will not escape me this time.

I once told her, if I burn, she'll die too. She didn't believe me then. I wonder if she does now.

"Where is he?" I say, voice deep and unrecognizable. The anger seethes from my tone, lashing at the trembling girl in my arms.

The others are screaming my name, begging me to stop. I ignore them.

"Tell me what you did!" I shout.

I feel the others at my back, hands pulling at my clothes,

but I do not budge. They can strip me bare, but I still won't release her. I will do what should have been done the moment Sofia came to Darkhaven.

I will kill her.

A hand is at the back of my neck, clenching tightly. The force angles my head upward and loosens my grip momentarily. Sofia is able to free herself with the help of my friends. I scream as she is torn from my grasp, and I claw at the air, desperate to cling to her for even a moment longer.

I am flung backward, and the space that separates me from the witch only increases as each second ticks by. I yell for Malik to release me, but he is ironclad. He believes I will not hurt him just to get to her, and he is right. But my weakness will be our downfall.

"Control yourself," Malik hisses into my ear, breath fluttering loose strands of hair.

Knowing I will not win by continuing to struggle, I fall limp, held securely in Malik's arms. Toe tips skidding across the hardwood floor, my body is pressed against his, each hard ridge jarring against my soft curves.

Sofia is across the room, huddled in a protective circle behind the others. Only Malik is by my side, but he has yet to release me.

He loosens his grip at my neck, allowing the soles of my feet to plant firmly on the floor, but he does not relinquish the arm wrapped around my torso. It remains hard, unyielding, so I lean against him, finding comfort in familiarity.

"Tell them," I shout. "Tell them what you did."

She shakes her head in disbelief. Eyes wide with fear, mouth open, unformed words and jumbled sentences spilling from her lips, she has the audacity to look at me as though I am the crazy one. Every second I stare at her, my animosity for this girl increases tenfold.

"Tell us what you did to him!" I scream.

I feel Malik falter, if only momentarily. His grip loosens around my waist, and I could take this as the perfect opportunity to free myself, but I don't. I will wait until he trusts me enough to let me go. His trust and Jasik's life are all that matter to me now.

"What is she talking about?" Malik asks, voice loud in my ear.

Hikari frowns and scans the room before looking at me.

"Where is Jasik?" she asks.

"He's missing," I say. "And the witch knows where he is."

"I don't!" Sofía shouts. "I swear, I don't."

"You lie!" I scream.

Malik drops me, and I quickly back away, putting space between myself and the others. I believe he would not harm me, but I can't be sure he is himself. The witch has too much control. She is too strong even for the hunters.

"Last night, I came here," I say. "I came here to ask for forgiveness and to tell you what I found out at the cave, about the rogue army. I saw you all. You were talking about me, about whether or not you can trust me."

"You didn't stay," Malik says. "Why? Because you thought we wouldn't forgive you?"

"I knew you would forgive me," I say. "After hearing what you said about destroying the amulet, I knew I could come back."

"What does this have to do with Jasik?" Malik asks. He turns and faces Sofía head on. "Where is my brother?"

"This has everything to do with him," I say. "You all had

no idea I was here. I stood in the foyer and listened to you talk about me, and you never saw me, never heard me."

"How?" Hikari asks.

"Magic," Holland says softly. He frowns, eyes blanking as he thinks about what he is saying. "Maybe an illusion spell. It is possible, but it would take a particularly strong witch to cast a successful spell on a house of vampires."

"What do you mean?" Jeremiah asks.

"In order for Ava to remain ... uh, *invisible*, for lack of a better term, the spell would have to influence everyone here," Holland says. "The stronger the target, the harder it is to hex. This means the witch would need to be stronger than the target. Or, at the very least, harness the magic of something *else* that is stronger."

"Like the full moon," I say, thinking about the night I met Jasik, the night he turned me into a vampire. "Witches often link their spells to the moon or the sun because they are both powerful, eternal energy sources."

"So you're saying Sofía spelled us last night?" Malik asks.

"That wasn't the first time either," I say. "She has been influencing you since she got here."

She gasps. "That is *not* true!"

"And you did it to me," I say. "You knew I would come back, and you saw the state I was in. You used my weakness against me. I had every intention of discussing this with them last night, but as soon as I got here, I forgot. In fact, I didn't think about you *at all*."

"How is that possible?" Hikari says. "You are a *hybrid*, and you have that damn amulet."

"She was exhausted," Holland says. "And starving. Think about how much magic she used that night just on us, and then she ran off and fought the rogues."

"I nearly died in the sun," I say, remembering the heat of the flames licking my skin.

"This made her weak, and her weakness made her vulnerable," Holland says.

"Not anymore," I say, gaze fixed on Sofía. "Tell me what you did to him, and maybe, I won't kill you."

"I swear," she says, arms up in retreat. "I don't know what you're talking about."

I exhale slowly, the sound loud and sharp in my mind.

"I'm sorry, but that's the wrong answer."

I step forward, decision already made, but Malik stops me. His eyes betray his inner conflict. He could release me. He could watch as I avenge my lover, his brother. Or he could be our leader. And a leader never breeds conflict. He stops it. Right now, with his eyes lost to his thoughts, he is suspended in time, unable to release me but unable to ask me to stop.

"Jasik is missing," I say when I return my focus to the witch. "If anything happens to him while you continue stalling—"

"Enough," Malik says, regaining his composure. He faces the girl. "Tell us what you know."

"I don't know anything," Sofía says, speaking each word slowly. "I had nothing to do with his disappearance. *I promise.*"

"You can understand why I don't believe you, right?" I say, voice thick with sarcasm.

"I did use my magic to influence you all," Sofía says. "And as I told Ava, I only did that to protect myself. She was hellbent on getting rid of me from the moment I got here, but I couldn't leave. Not until I found the rogue who killed my family."

"He's dead now, remember?" I ask.

"After he died, I realized I had nowhere to go," Sofía says.

"My sole purpose in life—to avenge my family—was fulfilled, and I like it here. I like all of you. I didn't want to leave, and I knew she would make me."

"So you *spelled* us?" Holland asks. "That is a cardinal rule you are never to break. You of all people should know that."

"I know," Sofía says. "And I am so sorry. Honest! I never hurt anyone. I just messed with your sense of reality a little. That's all."

Hikari snorts. "Oh, *that's all.*"

"I knew if Ava told you about our conversation last night, about how I spelled you not to hear us, you would have made me leave."

"I understand your reasoning," Malik says. "But you still should have given us the opportunity to make our own decisions. Friendship and family are not built on lies and manipulation. If you want our trust, you must earn it. You must *deserve* it."

"And *she* deserves it?" Sofía asks. "After *everything* she did to you, you are just going to welcome her back? I saved you all! If it weren't for me, she would have killed you that night."

Her words settle deep, sinking through flesh like a knife.

"She's right," I say softly. "The darkness would have made me kill you. All of you."

"*You're welcome,*" Sofía says flatly.

"I am grateful for what you did," I say. "If you hadn't been here to stop me, they would be dead right now. I couldn't live with knowing I caused them harm. This is a debt to you I can never repay."

"So you're not even going to try?" Sofía asks.

"No," I say plainly. "You did what you did, and I am grateful, but right now, my sire is more important to me than any of them. Now tell me where he is."

Sofía groans loudly.

"How many times do I have to tell you people? I have no idea where your boyfriend is."

I glance at Malik, who meets my gaze. With my eyes, I tell him everything he needs to know. My patience is running thin, and we are running out of moonlight. We haven't the time for games.

"What if he's still here?" Hikari asks. "What if we just can't see him?"

I shake my head. "He's not here."

"How do you know?" she asks.

"Because *I* would see him," I say. "Sofía isn't strong enough to hex me now."

FOURTEEN

We hear it in unison. The soft sound of someone approaching echoes all around us, but I know those feet don't belong to him. This person stomps, recklessly smashing the earth beneath his feet, making his presence known, whereas Jasik is swift and silent, an artist among amateurs.

He enters the house, feet smacking the hardwood rhythmically, and rounds the corner to the sitting room. But he doesn't enter the room. Instead, he leans against the door frame, hiking a foot up to rest against his other ankle. He is so casual about his intrusion, so confident.

The shock settles over us. We are stunned, paralyzed by the courage of a single rogue vampire. Not only did he locate our nest, but he had the audacity to enter uninvited, to challenge us in our own home.

He must have a death wish.

"I have a message," he says.

His voice is tainted by southern drawl. He fidgets with his hands, flicking at his overgrown nails. His eyes are blood red, his skin marked by death. He is dirty, and his stench permeates toward us.

Holland chokes on the foul odor, hacking as he takes in lungful after lungful. The others remain calm, voiceless.

"We have the vampire," the rogue says.

I suck in a sharp breath at the mention of Jasik, and I take a step forward in response. My body stiffens when Malik grabs my arm, halting my attack. I keep my vision focused solely on the rogue, but I feel Malik's eyes on me. In the silence, I can hear his plea. But patience has never been my virtue.

"Where is he?" I hiss.

"Your father has him," he says.

His words loop in my mind, and the room begins to blur as I process what this means. I knew when my father released me, there would be a cost, but I was confident I would be the one to repay that debt. It never occurred to me that freedom meant losing my sire.

This time, Malik steps forward, a hand still clasped around my arm, but the rogue silences him by waving him off.

"He will kill the vampire," the rogue says, and his confession slices straight to my core. "Come alone, with the amulet, or he dies."

Before I can respond, before even given the opportunity to question the rogue who stole my lover from our bed while I slumbered beside him, he does the unthinkable.

With deadly accuracy and using moves far too quick for my watery eyes, the rogue withdraws a stake from his jacket's inner pocket and plunges the tip into his chest. I hear every inch of wood burrowing through flesh. It sounds wet and sticky and *permanent*. He combusts before anyone can stop him.

Still, Malik tries. He lunges forward, reaching for the intruder only to be welcomed by death.

The wood stake drops to the floor, bouncing twice before rolling at a downslope. It now rests against the wall.

Our leader turns to face us again, but the anguish strewn

across his face is an unfamiliar sight. It masks his beauty with pain. His features, no longer fearsome and hard, are muddled and soft. He breaks eye contact to stare at his hands. They are cupped before him, cradling all that's left. The slight breeze from the open front door flutters the rogue's remains, and they swirl in the air before landing in a pile at Malik's feet.

"I have to go," I say.

I hear the words. I understand their meaning. But I don't remember saying them.

"You can't," Hikari says.

I don't respond to her. I remain focused on Malik, who is breaking into pieces before my eyes. Being the leader of a vampire nest can't be easy, and now, he must face his most difficult task. Either he saves his brother, thereby risking not just my life but the safety of the amulet and all that it entails, or he stops me, condemning his brother to death but likely saving this town by destroying this stone once and for all.

He must choose: his brother or the rest of the world.

He stares at me, lips quivering as he sucks in a shallow breath. He never speaks aloud, but his eyes say everything his lips cannot.

"I will get him back," I say. "And I will destroy this amulet."

"You'll die," Hikari says.

Finally, I look at the others, seeing them clearly for the first time in weeks. Ever since I took control of this amulet, I began to lose myself to its darkness. It might be silent now, but for how long? When will it waken? And when it does, will I be strong enough to stop it?

"Maybe that's how it should be."

The words hang in the air, the room silent. What surprises me most is my enemy—the witch—did not speak them. I did.

They escaped my lips before I even knew what I was saying. Everything about this night is surreal.

"Maybe I was never meant to survive that night," I say, mind lost to the moments I first met Jasik.

The full moon was bright overhead that night, and its light illuminated his silhouette in an eerie glow. Thinking back to the moment we nearly lost our fight, I remember little else. I close my eyes, and all I see is *him*. There was nothing but the moon's brightness, the darkness of his figure, and the crimson glow of his irises. And all are lost to me now.

"You would know," Malik says.

I blink several times, clearing my vision. My leader lowers his arms, releasing the ash remaining in his hands. It plops to the floor in a dusty heap.

"You would know if your sire is dead," he continues.

I think about the day Amicia died, about how her death affected the others. They were physically pained by her demise, by the severing of their link. They were weakened and emotional, near death and willing to die. I don't feel this way. I feel only my hatred for the witch and my fear of losing my lover.

"He's alive," I say, and Malik releases a sharp breath.

"You can't go alone," Hikari says.

"It is obviously a trap," Holland adds.

"But if she doesn't go, Jasik will die," Jeremiah says.

"I'll have the amulet," I say. My fingertips brush against its jagged exterior, feeling nothing within. "I can use it to destroy the nest."

"And if that doesn't work?" Hikari asks. "If that isn't enough to kill them all?"

Exasperated by her constant doubt and distrust, I resort

to shouting. She acts as though she doesn't even care if he perishes.

"Well, what do you recommend, then?" I ask. "Should I just let him die?"

"Of course not," she says. "We need to go with you. Going alone is suicide."

"Then he'll die for sure," I say.

"You don't know that," she says. "We've been doing this a long time, Ava. I think we can outsmart a few rogues."

"We might be able to circumvent the army, but we can't fool her father," Malik says. "Consider what we just saw. He has the power and control to convince a rogue vampire to take his own life. This . . . This is something I have never seen. We must be smart."

"Sure, he's strong, but—"

"There is no discussion here," I say, interrupting Hikari. "I go. You stay. That's it."

"You're just going to let her leave with the amulet?" Hikari asks, gaze focused on Malik.

"No one is *letting* me do anything," I say. "I *am* leaving, and no one here can stop me. As a courtesy, I am letting you know that I am taking this amulet, and I plan to use it to kill them all."

"It will consume your soul, Ava," Holland says. "And it will be too late. We won't get you back."

"I know."

"Do you?" he asks. "Do you know what that means?"

"It means you'll need to keep your word," I say. "Everyone in this room has pledged to destroy the amulet. If I can't do it on my own, if it . . . if it merges with me again, then the burden falls on you. You must destroy it. It contains too much power for one source."

"We will have to kill you," Holland says, voice whisper soft.

"I know."

"This is crazy," Sofía says in a huff.

I squeeze my eyes shut, jaw clenched, as I exhale slowly. Just the sound of her voice is enough to put me on edge. I might not be able to prove she had something to do with Jasik's abduction, but I am not swayed by her promises either. She knew. There is no other explanation for Jasik disappearing in the middle of the night, from a house full of vampires with heightened senses. We were spelled, and his cries for help fell on deaf ears.

"You can't possibly think taking that amulet straight to a vampire as powerful as him is a good idea," she adds. "Ava won't even have a chance to merge with it. He'll kill her and take the stone for himself."

"That does seem likely," Hikari says. "And then we'll be down a powerful ally."

"We're already down a powerful ally!" I yell. "Right now, Jasik needs me, and I won't abandon him. I won't leave him in that place."

"I'm not saying you *shouldn't* go," Sofía says. "I'm saying you need to leave the amulet."

"I can't say I'm surprised by your advice," I say. "You've been pining for this stone since you got here."

"Hardly," she says, voice deadpan. "The last thing I want is your precious rock."

"You are a hybrid, Ava," Hikari says. "With your powers and our skill, we can do this together—without that amulet. Just give us a chance."

"And risk Jasik's life in the process?" I ask. "I don't think so."

"His life is already at risk," Hikari shouts. "Yours doesn't need to be too."

"We should do this together," Malik says quietly. He speaks so low, I almost believe he didn't say anything at all.

"Isn't it interesting that you all so suddenly changed your mind and sided with the witch?" I ask. "How am I still the only one in this house who doesn't trust her?"

"This has nothing to do with the witch, Ava," Malik says. "I made this decision on my own. Losing you both and allowing the amulet to remain in a rogue's possession is too great a risk."

"And losing Jasik when my father discovers I didn't come alone is a risk you are willing to take?" I am baffled by his choices.

"Stop," Hikari says. "That isn't fair. Malik is cornered here, and you know it. Don't remind him how awful our situation is."

"Any decision I make is a difficult choice," Malik says. "But Jasik would want me to ensure the safety of you and that amulet. He would offer his life in exchange for yours, and I will respect that wish."

"This isn't up for debate," I say, knowing my argument is moot.

"You're right. It's not," Malik says. "Either we all go or no one goes."

In my bedroom, I listen through the door to the sounds permeating from downstairs. The others are still discussing how to best handle our situation. I knew we wouldn't compromise, so I left.

Focused solely on rescuing my sire, I dress quickly,

arming myself with everything I will need to save Jasik and exterminate the rogues once and for all: my dagger and the amulet.

Still, I am unconvinced the stone will do me any good. I feel nothing when I touch it except for the faintest hint of magic and darkness, though it remains mute when I summon it. For all I know, this thing is broken, but in case it isn't, I can't risk leaving it behind.

The others are blind to Sofía's deception, but I'm not. I see her for who she is: an impostor. We are sheep among wolves, and I don't particularly care for this twisted dynamic.

If the witch is strong enough to influence a nest of vampires—many who have been alive for centuries—she can't be trusted with this amulet too. She would be unstoppable.

I push aside the thick drapes and open my bedroom window. I maneuver onto the ledge, teetering between commitment and betrayal. With legs dangling over the edge, I swallow the knot that forms in my throat, feeling uneasy about this entire situation.

The vampires of this house know me well. They should expect such a daring move on my part, yet no one has come to check on me. No one has made sure I am even still here.

I think about what this means, about the effect of leaving them with the witch. She has already proven she can manipulate their thoughts and surroundings. They are vulnerable without me here to protect them.

But when I glance back at my vacant bed, sheets entangled at the foot board, I make my decision. I choose between him and them. If I am to lose my life, then I will do it saving Jasik's.

I leap, landing softly on the ground, and I am running. I dash through the forest, surrounded by silence. No one calls my name. No one tries to stop me. No one was even watching.

I am alone with the sound of my heavy breathing and my hammering heart. My legs burn as I nearly fly through the forest, but images of my father torturing my sire drive me forward.

Anger erupts in my chest, spilling past my lips in a loud roar. I scream, and with each bellow, the amulet at my chest begins to awaken. It feeds on my hatred, the stone burning against my cool skin.

FIFTEEN

I reach the cave, but I am alone.

I linger at the entrance—the very one that offered me reprieve only hours ago. Before, it was welcoming, a beacon of hope and freedom. Now, it suffocates me, stealing my life in a grip I cannot escape. I feel it even now, its fingers tethering around my neck, squeezing and smiling, webbing through the earth to pin my body in place so I cannot move.

The silence from within its belly wafts closer, like a scream—an ear-piercing, soul-crushing blare that is so loud it becomes all-encompassing. I can't remember what the world sounded like before that screech, before the quiet; the stillness is too much to bear.

I open my mouth, desperate to call to him, but no noise escapes. I try again, and I gurgle. Bubbles tickle the back of my throat, and I hack—but even that sounds strange. I don't sound like me.

The cave has no interest in my plea, so I too am silenced. Much like the deep, dark depths of the raging sea, this cave will offer mercy to no one.

I glance over my shoulder, feeling eyes at my back but seeing no one in the distance. The world is dark and depressive. Even the moon hides behind the clouds. I squint, but still, I see nothing.

The ground is streaked with blood, and in the dim lighting, it looks black. Ashes are scattered at my heels, and I don't know if either belong to *him*. To Jasik.

Maybe he is gone ...

The overwhelming fear that my sire *is* dead overtakes my sanity. My throat begins to close, and I focus on my shallow breath, on my heavy heart. I try to convince myself that he is okay, that I would know if he was dead. But inside, I am broken. The amulet used my anger and weakness to shatter everything I stood for. I am not the girl I used to be, and what if she is the only one with a connection to Jasik? If she is gone, he may be forever lost too.

I don't want to focus on all the things I have seen, all the nightmares that have haunted my sleep, but my mind will think about nothing else. In many of them, he turned rogue. My sire's daytime assurances that he would never relinquish his soul were never enough to fully convince me.

I think about Jasik being held captive by my father, the master of the soulless and the vile. If anyone could convince Jasik to release his humanity, it would be Papá. I saw a different side of him during my time in this cave. The man I once knew has become cunning and manipulative, someone eager to exploit another's deepest fears and darkest desires.

I must protect Jasik's soul at all costs—even if the price is my own. I owe him that.

I enter the black pit, slowly maneuvering my way through the tunnels I have come to know far too well. The smell is unimaginable—even worse than before. I fear what that means. Perhaps the decaying corpses have reached a new level of decomposition. Maybe there isn't anything to fear at all. Maybe nothing has changed—nothing but the arrival of a newcomer.

And yet, the stench makes my heart tremble in response. I try to still my nerves, to sate my anxiety, but nothing works. The deeper I descend, the more distressed I become.

I feel the eyes of a hundred rogues at my back, but when I spin in circles, weaving through the passageways like a fluttering butterfly, I am alone. I am not careful or calculated; I am reckless and foolish. My attempt at trickery, at overtaking this cave, is laughable. But I continue my search, determined to save my sire.

I stay close to the stone walls. They are jagged and sticky, often snagging the sleeve of my jacket. I feel the weight of my dagger against my breast, and it gives me comfort, even as my boots catch on the uneven ground.

I rest against the wall of a tunnel I am certain I have never passed through. It looks the same as the others, but the floor is becoming smoother, more compact and less rocky.

I walk slowly down the path, mindlessly reaching for the dagger. I don't withdraw it, but I leave my palm resting against the handle. The leather is scratchy against my skin, a harsh reminder of why I am here. I am not on a joy walk. I am here to kill or be killed. Nothing less. Nothing more.

The toe of my boot knocks against something hard, and I halt. I peer at it, unsure of what I am seeing. I crouch and brush my fingers against the uneven groove jutting up from the compacted dirt. It is cool and smooth.

As I chip away at what is likely decades of debris, I begin to unearth the structure. I shimmy farther and farther down the passageway, utterly oblivious to my surroundings but totally captivated by my discovery.

By the time I finish the small stretch, my nails are caked with dirt and my jeans are stained with mud, but I have cleared the path for a straight, thin block of metal. There are two—both parallel to each other, one on either side of the tunnel. Rotten wood planks connect each slab, and even though I have unveiled just a small section, I am positive it continues.

I am standing in a mining tunnel—one I never knew existed. I know very little about caves used for mining, but I am certain there are other entrances. If one section collapsed, those trapped inside would need another way out. That just seems like common sense. I have seen only one true entrance—the one I entered today—which means this system is vast, and Jasik might still be here. Perhaps I am not alone after all...

I continue hiking the passageway I just cleared, trekking through the remaining debris until the tunnel spills into a much larger room. This area looks similar to many of the other vast spaces I have encountered in this cave, except for a few glaring differences.

There are several mining carts and dozens of pickaxe tools.

The ground is smoother, and the tracks are cleared.

But the most noticeable difference is the walls themselves. Scattered among the slick, jagged rocks are glistening, shiny stones.

I approach cautiously with the intention of touching a stone, only to freeze. My fingers hover over the rocks, never quite connecting.

The better I inspect the crystals, the harder it is to overcome my dread at what this means. I know exactly what I am staring at, yet I am still dumbfounded by what I see.

This cave is comprised of black onyx crystals. They aren't everywhere, though. I see the spots in the walls that were chipped away, only to unveil useless rock. But there are still far too many to count.

I back away from the wall, fearful of touching a newly excavated stone. From my research, onyx has a great deal of power—one being the ability to steal immortality. A single measly crystal, like the one at my neck, might not be enough to grant me mortality, but a cave full of possibly interconnected black onyx might strip my powers. And I need my strength to rescue Jasik.

I exit the room through its most illuminated tunnel and shield my vision as I approach several bright lights. The abrupt difference makes my eyes water, but my senses quickly adjust.

The passage opens to another entrance. I exit, finding myself once again in the woods. The sky has cleared, and the moon and stars are shining brightly overhead. Something about this spot is familiar, yet I can't place it.

I hike a few feet from the opening, realizing that this cave exit doesn't lead me to a stretch of forest that no one travels. Instead, I find myself at the far edge of town, close to the bookshop and main street and the humans of Darkhaven.

I am positive there are more entrances like this, many of which probably lead to other parts of town, and this can only mean one thing.

My father did not choose to make his home base an old mining tunnel by accident. He knew what he was doing when he returned. He came to excavate those stones.

The day I was trapped by sunlight, he told me he returned with purpose. He made me believe he came back for me. Now I know the truth. He came for the crystals. Revenge against a town, and its people, that moved on without him is just his welcomed side effect.

His army is growing larger and stronger every day. Every

second he is allowed to remain in control of it is a risk we cannot take. His reign will be deadly, and if it isn't stopped, he will wipe out Darkhaven, killing the humans and witches who call it home.

I won't let that happen.

I glance back at the dark cave, knowing there must be dozens of tunnels I have yet to scour. Jasik might be in there, but if he's not, I can't waste time.

I take a step closer to the entrance I have just discovered and scan the street. From here, I can see the bookstore. The lights are on inside, and I wonder if I would be a welcomed guest. Luna has only showed me kindness, but that doesn't mean she will always be there to bail me out when I can't turn to my actual friends.

I gnaw on my lip, thinking about Jasik. If he isn't kept here, Luna might have seen or heard something. My father is keeping him *somewhere,* and I can only assume that place is in town. Where else will they ensure protection during daylight hours? Without coverage from within the cave, the woods pose too great a threat. Trees aren't ample coverage from the sun's deadly rays. That means they might have walked right past her store. If that's the case, she is lucky to be alive, and her luck could be my gain.

Before I can make my decision and emerge from the tree line, I am struck from behind. My vision blurs, starry lights bouncing behind my lids, and a high-pitched screeching noise bounces within the confines of my skull.

I fall to the ground, palms scrapping against the rough terrain, and my forehead smacks the sharp edge of a protruding rock. I am enveloped in darkness, but only momentarily. My eyes burn at the impact, and I suck in a lungful of loose soil. I hack, clawing at the ground to rise to my feet, only to be struck again and again.

I stop moving, but my stillness only encourages them.

I glance up, blood spewing down my forehead and seeping into the furrows around my eyes, just in time to see the sharp tip of a shoe. It makes impact, and my head is flung backward.

I am rolling, trying to move with the attack to cause the least amount of damage. I need to stay awake, to fight back, but every fiber of my body is protesting. The darkness is inviting, and for once, I am ready to welcome it.

Someone grabs me by the hair, dragging me to my feet, but only when I fully stand does my attacker release me. Something solid and flat strikes my torso, and I stumble backward. I slam against the outer wall of the cave, head smacking the rigid stone.

The pain is all-encompassing, yet I know I am not dying. This attack—so far—will not kill me. Still, each impact is excruciating. It is enough to make me think I might actually die, even if I know it isn't possible. Yet.

But everything stops. My attackers halt.

I am hunched over, blood pouring from a deep gash in my tongue. I let it cascade from my mouth, smearing down my chin and staining my clothes in a disturbing streak of red. I shiver. There is nothing quite like the sight of your own bloodshed.

I dare a peek, body straining to stand taller, to look stronger, and I stare into the dazzling eyes of four rogue vampires.

Somehow, even as I feel on the brink of death, my mind has the capability to wander, because as I stare at what should be some of the strongest creatures I will ever face, all I can think about is the amulet.

Because it is humming.

The stone sizzles, burning and radiating against my skin. Steady streams of power are seeping into my flesh, rejuvenating what is broken and bruised. It gives me strength and hope, and I believe I just might survive.

I look past my assailants and into the darkness beyond us, gaze settling on the black stones chipped from the walls of this cave. They glisten in the dim lighting.

From within the amulet, the entity wakes. It wakes because it has found its way home.

SIXTEEN

I summon the fire element. It aids me swiftly, as if it knows my situation is dire.

The abrupt change in temperature makes my skin crawl. As I wipe away the dew that drips from my temple, I consider withdrawing my dagger, but my hands are slick with sweat.

The misty air, hot and moist, quickly turns to a dense fog. I use the coverage to my advantage, dashing from where I stood to a spot several yards away.

The rogues have moved as well. I hear their soft footsteps in the damp soil. I inhale deeply, trying to use my heightened senses to locate the others, but the sweltering heat is all I can think about. It is sticky in my lungs, and I fight the urge to cough.

Unfortunately, before I can gather my bearings, a rogue vampire finds me first. He pounces from beyond the haze, and I don't see him until he has already lunged. We tumble to the ground, landing in a soft thud. Sinking into the earth, I can feel the soil ooze around my body, the mud mashing into a frame around us.

I hold him at a distance with one arm, frantically withdrawing my dagger with the other. I pull it free and plunge the blade into the rogue's chest. His eyes bulge as I slip it deeper into his torso. The moment I make impact with his heart, he combusts. His ashes scatter atop my soggy skin, and I spit cremains from my mouth.

I crawl to my feet, still hacking up gooey ashes. I spew the sludge from my mouth just as another rogue finds me. He slams into my body with such force the air is expelled from my lungs. The abrupt exhale makes a hissing sound in my chest and forces my body to jerk backward.

My head smacks against a tree, and I am caged in place within his ironclad arms. Dazed but well aware that I am in serious trouble, I smack my forehead against the rogue's nose. With blood gushing over his lips, he falters, but only momentarily.

Still, it is enough for him to sway backward, so I jab the heel of my hand forward to strike him in the throat. He wheezes, choking on his breath, so I hit him again. This time, I thrust upward with enough force to snap his neck. His head lulls backward as his body falls to the ground, seemingly lifeless. But I know he is still alive, so I drive my dagger into his heart.

I push away from the tree, squinting into the distance. There are two remaining rogue vampires, and I must find them first. I consider calling out, drawing them to me, but I can't risk facing both at the same time.

I stop abruptly when I see a figure. I am certain the silhouette belongs to another rogue vampire, but as I quickly make my way closer, her features become more prominent.

Luna.

The shopkeeper is several yards away, spinning in circles as though she too is lost in the fog. She turns so rapidly she doesn't even see me. I call her name, but my voice is lost to the wind.

Something catches my eye. A figure in the distance is approaching. She doesn't even see him. But I do, and this time, I recognize his crimson gaze.

A rogue vampire has spotted the girl. He smiles, fangs like death daggers meant solely for her heart. He rushes forward, and I scream her name again.

I rush to her side, leaping into the air. I soar past her and, with my dagger in hand, jump onto the rogue vampire. I cling to his body, wrapping my legs around his torso and flipping our bodies to the ground with a quick twist of my frame. As we fall to the ground, I stab at his back repeatedly.

She screams when he combusts. Having just witnessed me kill a rogue vampire, Luna backs away so quickly she falls to the ground. Her bottom sinks into the earth, but she still crawls backward.

"I won't hurt you," I assure her.

She screams again, but this time, she isn't looking at me. Instead, she points at something behind me.

I turn, facing the final rogue vampire. I sidestep, maneuvering so I stand between the girl and the monster.

"Stay behind me," I tell her.

With dagger in hand, I angle the blade so the moonlight glistens off the metal. It catches the eye of the rogue, who chuckles at my attempt to unnerve him.

I am growing tired. My control over the elements is draining too much power, so I decide to make this quick. I sheath my weapon, much to Luna's dismay. She squeaks her protest, but I ignore her. I don't need a weapon to kill him.

Instead, I focus all of my energy on projecting my magic. It swirls through the air, a solid beam of bright energy, targeted straight at his heart. It penetrates his sternum, leaving a devastating hole in its wake. He is gone before I even turn to face the girl.

I trudge slowly toward her. The heightened elements begin to dissipate, and the fog clears as I release them.

Luna stares up at me, and I offer her my hand. She takes it and brushes off her soiled pants after she stands.

"You saved me," she says.

I wave off her concern.

"Don't mention it," I say. "It's what we do."

"You protect people," she says.

I nod, thinking about the time I nearly killed her. I feel like an impostor, even though I know I wasn't myself that night.

"Your neck," she says.

I swipe at the amulet, fingertips grazing raw flesh. The stone has branded a mark on my skin. Already, I feel it healing. Revitalized skin is threading together, restoring what was damaged during the battle.

The amulet might have come alive when I truly needed it, but I didn't access its power. I faced four rogues, and I used only what was innate to me. I like to think that means I am making good progress. Malik will be proud.

She stares at the mark, eyes growing wider with each passing second. I know she is watching it heal before her eyes, and perhaps this is her breaking point. After all, there is a reason humans and vampires don't coexist. This might be too much for her.

"Are you okay?" I ask.

I hope I sound sincere, because I really do care about the girl. There aren't many people who would forgive someone after what I did to her, but she did. She even helped me—twice. Dare I say, she just might be a new friend.

She swallows hard and nods. She runs a hand through her tresses, and her hand gets caught in a tangle. With her fringe pulled back, I notice a faint scar on her forehead in the shape of a crescent moon.

"Thank you," she says.

"What were you doing out here anyway?" I ask.

"I was just out for a walk," she says. "I needed to clear my head, and then all of a sudden, I couldn't find my way back. The fog was so intense."

"Friendly tip, stay inside after dark," I warn.

She chuckles.

"Definitely wasn't the brightest decision I made this week," she agrees.

"Come on. Let's get you home."

"You know, when you said you would pay me back for the book, this wasn't exactly what I was expecting."

"No? Was this a bit too much?"

"Just a tad," she says. "I mean, the book didn't cost *that* much."

"I'm just glad I repaid that debt," I say, grinning.

SEVENTEEN

I sense their presence before I hear their approach. They are swift, like whispers that ravage as wildfires. They are silent, like shadows clawing across pavement. One minute, Luna and I are alone. The next, we are surrounded by vampires.

Her eyes are wide, her heart overworked, and she reeks of fear. It is a stagnant odor that I taste at the back of my throat. But she is human, so my instincts react. My stomach grumbles, fangs throb. I shake and quiver from the excitement building within.

As though she can hear my inner turmoil, Luna looks at me. Her eyes plead with me for her survival. She is concerned for her safety, and she silently begs for my protection.

"Luna," I begin, gaze darting between the shopkeeper and the vampires, "these are my friends."

She offers them a weak smile, but her fear does not subside. They will need to prove themselves to her—just as I have. Then again, I nearly killed her a few nights ago, so I imagine introductions won't go well.

"We assumed you would need backup," Hikari says, voice deadpan, utterly ignoring the human beside me. She doesn't bother even looking at Luna.

"Rash and disobedient," Jeremiah says. "Sounds like Ava."

He smiles, and my heart melts. But the moment is brief, and before I know it, he frowns, his ironclad exterior once again separating us. But he was playful, even if only for a moment, like the vampire I used to know. He joked, and he smiled, and for the shortest second of my life, Jeremiah was my friend. Again. This gives me hope that he will one day forgive my misdeeds.

"I suppose confessing my disappointment in your actions would be moot," Malik says.

"I'm not sorry," I say.

"I'm not surprised," he counters.

"Not only did you disobey a direct order from your elder, it appears you did so in vain," Malik says.

"You didn't find Jasik?" Jeremiah asks.

I shake my head, unable to speak the words aloud. I don't miss the surprise in Jeremiah's voice when he asks me this. We were confident Jasik would be here. My father's patsy told us so. I guess we were misled.

"But you did find something," Malik says, gaze settling on Luna.

With emotionless eyes, he scans the length of her body, taking in her thin frame, her pale skin, her wild hair, her oval eyes. I am used to this side of Malik—the part of him that's all about business—but Luna isn't.

I imagine he looks unnecessarily scary to her eyes.

She surprises me, summoning a rush of courage rarely seen in mortals. Luna narrows her eyes at my leader, and I find strength in her defiance.

"I am not a *thing*," she says. "I'm a person."

Malik fights a smile—badly so—and clears his throat. He stares at her for a long moment, as if seeing her clearly for the first time, before focusing his attention on me. I wish he'd just keep looking at her . . .

"I asked you not to leave," he says.

"I asked you not to come," I counter.

"Ava," he scolds. Only my mother could say my name with such disdain.

"You know I had to," I say. "And I would rather not waste time justifying the decision I made. It's done. I can't take it back, so let's move on."

"I agree that time is fleeting," he says. "But we will discuss your actions at a later time."

I roll my eyes, groaning internally. I consider a snippy response, like how it isn't my fault that they failed to predict the obvious choice I would make. They know me well enough to know I would sneak out. I have done it before, and I will probably do it again. He is acting as though he doesn't know me at all.

"How many are left?" Malik asks.

He scans the dark opening to the cave, which is now several yards behind us, but he doesn't remain focused for long. His gaze lingers to Luna the moment she glances over her shoulder. With everyone but me looking at the entrance to the cave, Malik eyes the human cautiously. I understand his captivation with her. I feel the pull too. There is something about this girl that is special, alluring. I can't describe it, but I have felt this way for no other human.

"All of them," I say, pretending I don't notice his interest in her. "Except four."

It takes a moment for my words to process, but I see the exact moment he hears me. He blinks several times, the haze in his eyes clearing. Malik frowns, his brow furrowing in confusion. Finally, we make eye contact.

"There were only four here?" Malik asks.

"I only came across four," I explain. "There might be more. This cave is vast. It was used for mining."

"Mining?" Malik asks.

He stares at the ground, lost in thought. I have never seen him so distracted, so interested in all the little details that don't revolve around his inner circle. He is fascinated by Luna, even if he will never speak those words aloud, and now he is showing keen interest in the use of this cave. Maybe he knows more than he was letting on.

"Did you know they did mining in Darkhaven?" I ask.

"Yes, but that was almost two hundred years ago," he says. "Darkhaven has never been an active mining town. In fact, the tunnels were supposed to be sealed off."

"Well, they weren't," I say. "And I can't be sure how much of it I still haven't explored. Just because I didn't find him doesn't mean Jasik isn't still in there."

"But if he isn't being held in the cave, we will waste what little time we have left before sunrise," Hikari says.

"We could separate," Jeremiah suggests. "Ava can continue exploring the tunnel, Hikari can take the forest, and I can check the town."

"Wh-What should I do?" Luna asks, stuttering.

The vampires fall silent, all staring at her curiously. We have spent the last several months desperately trying to bridge the gap between mortals and immortals, but the witches of Darkhaven turned us down time and time again. We assumed humans wouldn't be able to handle the existence of magic and vampires and all things that go bump in the night. Maybe we were wrong. Maybe we were trying to befriend the wrong mortals.

"We can't separate," Malik says, speaking each word slowly. His gaze never leaves Luna's.

"Because?" Jeremiah asks.

"We need to stick together," he says. "Separating is too risky. Ava's father has the upper hand here. We need to be smart about our attack."

"Where are the others? Holland? And the witch?" I ask. I clear my throat. Just thinking about her leaves a bitter taste in my mouth. "Maybe they can help."

"They are helping," Jeremiah says. "They're at the manor. Researching."

"Researching?" I question.

The amulet begins to hum, but the sound is muffled by the wind. I think only I hear it—until Luna glances at it and frowns. The others don't seem to notice.

"It appears Holland might have found a way to properly destroy the amulet," Malik says.

"Really?" I ask, breathless. My excitement surprises even me. "How?"

Malik glances at Luna, who silently watches our conversation unfold. Besides offering to help find a vampire she barely met, she has remained mute. Still, her presence is powerful. It's obvious everyone feels it.

"Perhaps we should speak about this in private," Malik suggests.

"Oh, I—uh, I can leave," Luna says, still stumbling over her words.

"She's cool," I say, drawing a wide, genuine smile from the girl. "She knows."

Malik exhales sharply, slowly, and squeezes his eyes shut. He takes several seconds to adjust to this new information before opening his eyes again. His gaze finds me.

"Do you have any idea how irresponsible you are? How difficult you make it to be your leader?" he asks, shaking his head. "One rule. We have one cardinal rule that mustn't be broken, and you can't even abide by that. I am far too lenient with you, Ava. You know this."

"I didn't tell her," I say, instantly defensive. "She ... just found out."

"How?" Malik asks. "And the story I am looking for is one that doesn't involve you *at all*. In fact, I want to hear that she was aware of our existence all along."

"She's the girl ..." I clear my throat, searching for the words least likely to anger him further. "She, uh, she—"

"Ava almost ate me," Luna says with a soft chuckle. Her grin immediately disappears. "It sounds weird when you say it out loud."

Malik exhales again, just as loud and overdramatic as all the other times he has expressed his disappointment in me, and scratches at his head. His hair is longer now. Usually, it is buzzed close to his skull, but it looks like he hasn't kept up with it in at least a couple of weeks. I imagine a million different forms of punishment are looping through his mind, bouncing around that very skull. I wonder which he will choose.

"You really are impossible, Ava," Malik says.

There is the tiniest hint of humor in his voice, like I am so disobedient, I am actually fun to have around. But with anything, there is a limit, and I tread that very fine line far too often.

"The last thing we need to worry about right now is the girl," I say. "Jasik is still missing. We need to get him back. He can't spend another night with ... with *him*."

Malik's jaw clenches, the tiny muscles in his cheek contracting. He is upset—frustrated that I have allowed a human to discover the existence of magic and angry that his brother is still being held hostage by a raging lunatic—but he knows I am right. And at this point, we can use all the friends we can get, especially the mortal ones—those who can walk in daylight.

"I am still unconvinced Jasik isn't here," I say. "My father chose this mining cave for a reason."

"Maybe because it was large enough to house an army of rogue vampires?" Hikari asks.

"I found something," I say.

"What?" Malik asks, tone harsh and serious.

"They have been mining for stones," I say. "I must have come across dozens of onyx crystals."

"You think this is why he has gathered his army here?" Hikari asks. "For the stones? I thought he came for you."

"I thought so too. But that had to be a lie, because I refuse to believe this is a coincidence."

"I'm not sure we can go as far as to say he lied," Malik says. "I imagine he wants both—the stones and your power."

"Why would he want these crystals anyway?" Jeremiah asks. "I thought the only reason yours was so special is because of that *thing* inside."

This catches Luna's attention. She frowns, squinting to see the amulet more clearly. Instinctively, I move away, turning so she can't focus well enough on the darkness swirling within.

"Black onyx is very rare," I say.

"Or maybe it isn't rare," Hikari asks. "Maybe no one knew where to look. Maybe these stones have been here all along."

"Black onyx is a particularly powerful stone," Luna says.

"The books you bought from my store should shed some light on their innate power."

"Her store?" Malik says. "You visited her store? When?"

"Twice," Luna says with a smile.

"Was this before or after the attack?"

"Both, technically," Luna says.

I glare at her, and she silences. Luna mouths an apology, but she does this in front of Malik, who now probably thinks I have more to hide. Honestly, I don't think this night could get any worse.

"Ava... I..." Malik trails off, shaking his head, stunned silent.

"Look, I know I've broken your rules, but you said we'd talk about that later," I say. "Right now, we need to find Jasik and annihilate this army before he releases it on the town."

"Agreed," Hikari says.

"Yes," Malik says, exhaling sharply. "If we don't—"

"There will be nothing left," Jeremiah says, interrupting his leader.

"But how?" Hikari asks. "There are too many of them. This isn't a fight we can win."

"We have the advantage, right?" I ask.

"What advantage?" Hikari asks.

"He might have a rogue army, but we have two powerful witches, three several centuries- old vampires, a hybrid, and an amulet with the power of an entire coven—"

"Plus a little extra," Jeremiah says bluntly.

"And when we find Jasik, we'll be up another vampire," I say.

"We just need to find a way to quickly kill a lot of vampires," I say.

"Yeah," Hikari says with a fake smile and shrug. "I mean, how hard could that be?"

"Maybe Holland can help," I say. "He might know of a spell or something."

"I'm guessing if Holland knew of a spell powerful enough to kill a bunch of rogues at once, he would have mentioned something last night," Hikari says.

"Besides, he's been so focused on the amulet," Jeremiah says. "I doubt he's spent time researching the army."

"There has to be a way," I say. "We have magic at our disposal. There is nothing magic can't do as long as you have a witch strong enough to cast the spell. Technically, we have three."

"Perhaps this is true," Malik says. "But we need time to research, to write a spell strong enough to beat his army."

I kick at the ground, never before feeling as defeated as I do in this very moment. Somewhere out there, Jasik is desperate for his freedom, and he is running out of time. The great irony is we are all immortal. Time is the one thing we are supposed to have in abundance.

"I, uh…" Luna says. She clears her throat. "I think I have something that can help."

EIGHTEEN

The walk back to Luna's shop is quick and silent, each step and passing second torturous. I can focus on nothing else but her assurances. She sparks hope among the desperate and pessimistic. I am not sure Luna understands just how important this is. Not only could she help us rescue Jasik, but she could save this town too.

We wait at the counter while Luna disappears into the darkness at the back of her shop. I already know where she is going. There is a doorway that leads to her storage room, and that is where she keeps her most valuable relics and tomes. Every time I have sought help, she has returned from that room with the information I needed. I can only hope she has the key to ending all of this.

Even though she has done nothing for me to doubt her, I am antsy. I tap my fingers against a glass showcase, the beat of a mousy tune radiating through my bones.

My imagination runs wild, forcing me to remain a bystander while a million different scenarios play out in my mind. The outcome of every single one is dire and catastrophic. It leaves a bitter taste in my mouth.

In the course of only a few minutes, it feels as though several hours have passed. I peer out the window, but even though I expect to see the sunrise, the street is dark and deserted. It is still night. We still have several hours before we must halt our search for Jasik.

Malik places a calming hand to my shoulder, but it does not quell my anxiety. I am well aware that my entire body is shaking. My foot is bouncing against the hard floors, sending shockwaves through the wood. My fingers drum loudly against the countertop, echoing through the tiny storefront. I am breathing loudly, sucking lungful after lungful through my nose in long, deafening streams. The noise is a distraction I so desperately need.

"He will be okay," Malik says.

I shake my head, feeling the burn in my eyes. My vision begins to blur, but I blink several times to clear my sight. When I exhale, my breath quivers. My lungs shake, body convulsing.

The stress of not knowing what is happening or how this will end is a torment I have never before experienced. I have no idea where my sire is. I don't know if he is dead or alive, if he is vampire or rogue. But I know he needs me, and that makes waiting so much harder.

"We don't know that," I whisper.

"You must remain strong," Malik says. "For him."

I turn, facing the others. Hikari and Jeremiah mirror my somber expression. Like me, they too fear the worst. But Malik stands tall and strong, a true leader on the brink of tragedy. I suppose his emotionless state makes sense. Death and war are what he knows best. To him, this is just another day in Darkhaven. But it shouldn't be this way. This town shouldn't be soaked in bloodshed.

Luna returns, carrying a thick tome in her hands. She rounds the counter, standing beside the register. She sets down the book but leaves her palms covering the front in a protective embrace. She glances at me, and I see her hesitancy.

"You have to promise you will return this to me unharmed," Luna says.

"You have my word," I say.

She nods and swallows loudly. Finally, she removes her hands, offering our first glimpse at the text. Immediately, I know this is a grimoire—a book of shadows passed down through generations. Typically, this contains witchcraft spells, magic elixir recipes, and anything else that might help a witch perfect her craft. I have never seen one in the hands of a human.

It smells musty and stale, like it has been around far longer than Luna has. The book is crafted from brown leather, with a pentagram pressed into the front cover. It is thick, with heavy binding to contain the crinkly, tea-stained pages within. It appears to be on the very brink of disarray, like at any moment the binding will unweave and the pages will scatter.

"This was my grandmother's book," Luna says. "And it belonged to her grandmother before her."

"I guess the belief in magic skips a generation," I say with a chuckle, but I chastise myself immediately. Now is not the time for jokes or lightheartedness.

"I didn't know my parents," Luna says. She smiles softly, but it is bleak. It never reaches her eyes.

"Are you a witch?" Hikari asks. Her gaze flutters between the tome and the girl.

"No, but I do come from a family of believers," she says. "My grandmother used to tell me stories about magic. She was confident there was more to this world than the mundane."

"She was right," Malik says.

Luna nods, eyes lost momentarily. I wonder what she sees when she thinks about her past. Does she see a supportive family who would die for her? Or is she alone now because she was abandoned then, cast away as useless, deemed an abomination, like so many other orphans? My heart breaks for her. I found a new family. She didn't.

"My grandmother used to tell me there was so much evil in this world, too much for one planet," she says. "She said there had to be a reason for it, because people are supposed to be good. She thought something must be making them bad."

"Where there is light, there is darkness," I say. "The world needs both."

"Well, she was convinced good was being influenced by bad, so she kept this book in the family, adding what she could, what she thought might one day help us."

"Help you?" Malik asks.

"She wanted me to have this in case I were to ever encounter it," Luna says.

"It?" Hikari asks.

"Magic. Evil. The darkness she believed was lurking around every corner."

"Vampires," Malik clarifies. "This darkness, it was vampires?"

"Or witches," Luna says. "We believed in it all, and she believed both could be evil."

"And this is why you—a mortal—have a spell book?" Malik asks.

I can tell he doubts her story. Malik has been alive a lot longer than most vampires, and in all the years he has fought to protect this world, he has probably never encountered a human like Luna. But he has honed his senses, his intuition, and right now, I am sure his cautionary lights are blaring. I find it annoying because he never feared the witch.

"Believers tend to collect things," Luna says. She glances over her shoulder, looking at her store. "I suppose that's why I opened Lunar Magic. I like being around this stuff."

"You can understand my hesitancy," Malik says. "We have only just met you, and so far, you seem to have the tools we need every time we need them. We don't fancy coincidences in our line of work."

"It's not uncommon for mortals who believe in magic to keep relics, to research the supernatural," Luna says, a bit defensively. "It's what we do. Like bibliophiles who have their own library or gamers who own every console, even the ones they don't play on."

"She's right," I say. "By nature, humans have an unhealthy obsession with the occult."

"Just look at Hollywood," Jeremiah says with a snort. "I mean, how many times have they remade *Dracula*?"

"I understand that," Malik says. "But you aren't merely obsessed. You just happen to have some pretty rare texts lying around. That is cause for concern."

"That's all Lunar Magic," she says, hiking a thumb over her shoulder to point at the back of the store. "I purchase these things for the shop on a regular basis. I keep some. I sell others. Because I would rather have these things in my possession, where I know they are safe, than out on the streets, being sold to someone who shouldn't have access to this kind of power."

"She isn't a threat," I say, tone far harder than intended. My annoyance is growing—as is my anxiety. We don't have time to justify Luna's back story.

"I wouldn't be helping you if I were a threat," she adds.

"You must understand, we encounter far more foes than allies," Malik says.

"I know," she says. "But I just want to help."

"And how can you do that?" Hikari asks. "How can this book help us?"

Luna smiles and opens it. The spine cracks, but she is careful as she maneuvers through it, gently allowing the text to lie flat on the countertop. The pages are stiff and brittle, and as she works her way past each one, she gnaws on her lower lip. Her eyes are narrowed, brow furrowed in concentration. Finally, she stops and looks at me, hopeful.

"This is it," Luna says.

The book is still facing her, but I can scan the page contents. The entry is handwritten, and since it is at the back of the book, I believe it was written by her grandmother. I read the title aloud.

"The Orb of Helios?" I question.

"It is strong enough to channel the power of the sun," Luna says. "So few crystals have that much innate strength. Most would crumble under the weight of it."

"I've never heard of it," I say slowly.

"Well, maybe you can use it to, you know." She waves her arms around, fisting the air dramatically.

"To?" Hikari asks. She looks as confused by the gesture as I am.

"To blow up all the bad guys," Luna says in a huff. "Or something. You know, all at once."

"I mean, that would be ideal," I say. "Killing them all at once, but I would need a spell to go along with this. Channeling the sun isn't easy. It is more powerful than the moon, making it that much harder to summon and harness and contain."

"Perhaps Holland and Sofía could assist," Malik says.

"I'm sure you three are savvy enough to create the spell

you would need," Hikari adds.

"Well, sure, but even though creating a spell that would actually work would be hard, that isn't the most difficult part," I say. "I would need this Orb of Helios, and since I have no idea what that is, I am guessing it will be particularly difficult to find. We don't have time to research it, to figure out where we might find one."

Luna smiles brightly, a Cheshire Cat grin that morphs her features into an eerie gleam. Her eyes are dazzling. The excitement practically oozes from her body.

She grabs a small brown box from behind the counter and places it beside the book. She turns it around so the latch faces me, and she flicks the metal hinge with her finger. It opens.

Inside, a small sphere is surrounded by glossy, white silk. It rests at the center of the box. About the size of my palm, the orb is glowing, and the light inside the crystal is mesmerizing. It glistens like glitter and hums like magic. The bright, shining light swirls round and round, constantly moving, vibrating within its glass shell.

"I told you I could help," Luna whispers.

"Luna, where did you get this?" I ask, voice just as soft.

"My grandmother befriended a woman who claimed to be a witch," she says. "They were close, and the witch gave her this orb, claiming it would keep her safe. She said it would protect us against evil."

"And you just kept it this whole time?" I ask. "You never used it?"

"We aren't witches," Luna confesses. "We could never access the magic inside. Even though we couldn't harness its power, I knew others could. So I saved it. Like I save everything."

I let my fingers hover over the orb, never making contact. I fear what might happen if a vampire touches it, but still, I am drawn to its power, to the erratic swirling of magic within. It reminds me of the amulet, of the darkness inside. And just like the entity, this orb calls to me, reaching out, desperate to make a connection. It is hungry for freedom, just like the entity.

"I won't be able to bring this back," I admit. "The spell, I am sure it will consume the orb. It'll be gone forever."

"I know," Luna says. "But I believe in fate. I think I was meant to keep this orb, meant to help you and your friends."

Luna closes the box, severing the connection and silencing its siren call. I blink several times, clearing my vision, but I still see the bright lights behind my lids. I still hear its muffled cry.

"Thank you," I say, meeting Luna's eyes.

"You're welcome," she says. "I just hope it helps."

"It will," I say. "I know it will."

She closes the book, but her hand lingers on its cover, fingers trailing the outer edge of the pentagram. Finally, after a long moment, she slides the tome toward me and places the box containing the orb on top of it.

"I guess this means I owe you again," I say with a chuckle. "Another debt to be repaid."

I grab the book and box, holding the text close to my chest with one arm and safely securing the box in my other. They are side by side, and I tighten my grasp around them, confident it would take an army of a thousand men to free them.

"Just save our village," she says. "That's more than enough for payment."

NINETEEN

The manor is silent when we enter. The tome is heavy in my arms, the box jutting into my chest, but they are nothing compared to the weight of the air in this house. That is suffocating.

A sense of dread washes over me, and with it, there is an urgency I can't shake. The stillness has seeped into my core, and the silence screams a truth that is hard to hear.

We made it home, and now, we are one step closer to rescuing Jasik, to facing a rogue army, to killing my father. By sunrise, the world will look entirely different, but I am not so sure I will be alive to see it.

We find Holland and Sofía sitting on the floor in the parlor, surrounded by stacks of books. Both appear entranced by what they're reading. So captivated, they haven't even noticed our arrival.

Jeremiah reaches Holland's side and sinks beside him. Their eyes meet, and the relief is so strong, so overpowering, it practically becomes a tangible force.

Jeremiah looks at his lover longingly and places a soft kiss to his forehead. Holland closes his eyes and leans into Jeremiah's embrace, and my heart nearly implodes from my desire for Jasik's touch. But I worry I may never experience it again.

Something about this night has me on edge, and I can't quite place the reasoning behind my instinctual fear. I try to remain focused on the new plan, on the spell that will surely work.

They pull away, and Holland looks at me, eyes hopeful and searching the room for the missing member of our family. I shake my head, unable to say the words aloud. Jasik is not with us. I failed to find him, to bring him home. Holland frowns at the realization, but his gaze settles on the relics in my arms.

"We found something," I say.

I allow myself to be hopeful that Luna is providing the answer we so desperately need. My optimism changes my tone, and my tone changes the feel of the room. The tension eases, and I am able to easily suppress the nagging sensation that something is wrong.

I close the space between us, gently setting both the book and box on the floor. Sofía is beside me, less than an arm's length away, and while I do not like her—nor do I trust her—I am willing to overlook the uneasiness in my gut whenever she is near if that is what I must do to save Jasik. I can set aside my pride—but can she?

"What do you know about the Orb of Helios?" I ask Holland.

Sofía visibly stiffens beside me. Holland notices too. His gaze flicks to her, and he frowns. But no one mentions it.

"It's a myth," he says slowly, eyes still on Sofía.

"Is that all you know?" I ask.

He tears his vision from hers to look at me again.

"Supposedly, it is a crystal strong enough to contain the sun's energy," he adds.

"Have you ever seen one?" I ask.

He shakes his head.

"I have read about it, but it is believed not to be real," he says. "I don't know anyone who has seen one in person."

I slide the box toward him, and he stares at it for a long time. No one moves, not even Holland. He simply looks at the box, perhaps too scared to actually open it. His breathing grows louder, as do the steady beats of his heart. Both drown out my own.

"We found one," I whisper.

"Is it ... Is this—"

"The Orb of Helios," I confirm.

He touches the box and sucks in a sharp breath. Maybe he too feels its pull. Maybe all witches can. He hesitates, much like I did, but his fear of its power is nothing compared to mine. That orb may very well steal my life. But Holland should be safe.

Gently, he opens the box, letting the lid fall back as far as the hinges will allow. The orb is so bright it illuminates the darkened room. The magic swirls within the glass and dancing lights spread across the ceiling.

Once again, I am captivated by the essence stored inside. Its pull is stronger than before, and this time, I am unable to fight the urge to touch it. I reach out, fingers nearly making contact. Holland stops me, his grip strong. His hand covers my own, and he squeezes me tightly.

"Don't," he warns. "We can't predict its power."

I pull back, distancing myself from the crystal. I am embarrassed by my lack of control. But something about this sphere calls to me more than it does to the others, because none of them move to touch it. They don't seem to be as bewitched as I am.

"We can use this against the rogue army," Holland says. "But we must be careful. You can't touch it. Ever. Not until we know how powerful it actually is."

I nod. He's right. I was careless. I must remain in control of my own body.

"We have to write a spell first," I admit. "I have a grimoire. Maybe there is something inside that can help."

I tap the book, and Holland tears his gaze from the orb to look at the book of shadows I have placed beside him. His fingers graze the worn leather.

"Where did you get this?" he asks.

I eye Sofía cautiously and decide to provide as little information as possible. The last thing I want to do is risk Luna's safety. I can't protect her if I am searching for Jasik.

"It was a gift from a friend," I say carefully.

"I'll read it, cover to cover," Holland says. "I know this can work, Ava. We can bring him home."

Holland grabs the orb, carefully cradling it in his hand, and I gasp at the sight of it outside of the box. I am desperate to touch it, to connect with the energy inside, but I don't move. I maintain my composure, hanging on to Holland's promise that we will reunite with Jasik soon enough.

"This is really going to work," Holland says, voice giddy with excitement.

Several hours have passed since Holland began researching the Orb of Helios, and with each passing second, we are closer to daylight, to losing our opportunity to bring Jasik home alive.

As he promised, Holland read Luna's grimoire cover to

cover, spending the last hour drafting a spell that he is confident will harness the sun's energy and eliminate my father's rogue army once and for all.

"The spell will summon the power of the sun and channel that energy through this orb," Holland explains.

"That will be strong enough to kill the entire rogue army?" Malik asks.

"In theory, yes," Holland says.

"In *theory*?" Hikari asks. "I don't like the sound of that."

"We are talking about a ritual that likely has never been done before," Holland says. "I hate to say it, but I am making this up as I go. I can make no promises, but this *should* work."

"If anyone can make it work, it's you," I say.

Holland smiles at me, and I see it. That rush of confidence that words alone can provide. He sits taller, speaks louder.

"There is one minor detail that is pretty important," Holland says.

"What is it?" Malik asks.

"The orb will channel the sun's energy, cascading light all around," Holland says. "This is how the rogues will die. It will be just as strong as the daytime sun."

"That's good, right?" I ask. "That means it will work."

"It will kill *every* vampire in sight," Holland says. "Including all of you."

I suck in a sharp breath and hold it. That means we can't be present, which makes performing the spell harder and more dangerous. How are we to free Jasik if we can't be there?

"Sofía and I are the only ones capable of performing this spell," Holland says. "And whoever isn't performing the sun spell will be performing the spell to destroy the amulet."

I frown, surprised we are still talking about the amulet. I

assumed we were focused solely on the army, on Jasik, on my father.

"We're doing both?" I ask. "At the same time? Is that safe? We are talking about a lot of energy at one time."

"That energy overhaul is exactly what we need to destroy the amulet," Holland says. "It's the only thing that will destroy the entity and safely remove the coven's stored magic. It has to be done at the same time."

"I know you want to find Jasik and stop this army," Sofía says. "But destroying the amulet is just as important."

"I know," I say, but I don't look at her. I remain focused on Holland.

"It's getting stronger again, isn't it?" Sofía asks.

I nod slowly. I opt for honesty, but I am frustrated that *she* is the only one who noticed.

"It is," I say softly. "That's why I agree that this is important. I can't lose control again, and now that we have the orb and the sun spell, I don't need the amulet to save Jasik."

"I am going to perform the sun spell, Ava," Holland says. "It's much more complicated, and Sofía and I agree that I am the stronger witch."

"Good," I say. "That's good. I trust you."

I don't care that my words might hurt Sofía's feelings or frustrate my nestmates. After this is over, if she truly isn't a burden in everything we must do, if she keeps her word and helps us, I will apologize. I will give her a chance. I will let her stay.

"That means you need to give Sofía the amulet," Holland says slowly.

Instinctively, I clasp the amulet in my hand, shielding it from his words. The stone burns against my palm. The entity within is angry. I can *feel* its protest, but it isn't strong enough to stop me. Not right now. But I know, in time, it will consume my soul. Like before, it will get stronger, and I will get weaker. This is my chance to be free of this burden, but relying on Sofía—a stranger I do not trust—with the power inside isn't easy. I just hope we aren't all making a grave mistake.

I exhale sharply, summoning the strength to be rid of it, and I yank. I break the chain, feeling an abrupt snap with the darkness inside. Even in its weakened state, it still surrounded me, but I have severed that connection, broken its power over me. Now, I am in control.

I hold out the amulet, the chain dangling from my hand. Sofía smiles at me, but something in her eyes makes my stomach twist. My gut objects to her alliance, much like the entity fights our disconnect.

Her hand is open, her palm facing upward beneath mine, and it takes every fiber of my body working as one, but I do it. I unclench my fist. I let go. The stone falls, gravity now in control, and the moment the crystal is safely tucked in her grasp, everything changes.

"I was beginning to think he was wrong," Sofía says, voice laced in malice.

"W-Who was wrong?" I ask, stuttering.

"Your father," she says.

Time nearly stops. Her confession leaves me dizzy and lightheaded, like I am floating away, but the echo of my comrades' gasps cement me in place.

I was right.

Sofía is evil.

"He assured me you would offer the stone in exchange for the vampire," she says. "But I'll be honest, I'm surprised it took this long. I'm not convinced you two have a real future after all."

"Is that a threat?" I hiss. "If you hurt him, I swear—"

She waves off my concern with a chuckle.

"I knew you couldn't be trusted," I say.

"You did," she says. "When I used magic on your nest that first night, I worried I might have overplayed my hand. After all, I needed them to trust me in order for his plan to work. And while that rogue attack was unexpected, it worked in my favor. You see, everyone was so focused on *you*, they forgot to worry about *me*."

"You never came for the rogue," I say.

"Wow, you're a clever one, aren't you?" she says, condescendingly.

"Did you kill your coven?" I ask.

"I did what I had to do to prove my allegiance."

"You did this for *him*?" I ask. "For my father?"

"Can I tell you a secret?" she asks, voice whisper soft. "I killed yours too."

I gasp, but instead of anger, I am overwhelmed by agony. Had I not hexed my coven, they could have stopped her. I will never be free of my guilt for my part in all of this.

"Of course, I didn't do it alone," she says. "But I think you know that. You know exactly who killed them and why they had to die."

"You're in a house full of vampires," Hikari says, seething. "You'll never make it out with that amulet."

She laughs, deeply, a raw and hungry sound, and it makes me weak in the knees. She doesn't even look like herself anymore. It's as though she is morphing from the picture of a weak, lonely witch to something far more sinister.

"You know what you did to these vampires?" Sofía asks, eyes on me. "You made them weak. Your ridiculous desire for peace made them forget they have real enemies in this world. They risked their own immortality for a chance to please you. You warned them over and over about me—a *true* enemy—and they refused to believe you. That wouldn't have happened if you hadn't made them weak to your cause."

I lunge, taking the opportunity to catch her off guard, but she quickly thwarts my attack. She moves faster than I do. I blink, and she is gone. Standing behind me, her breath is hot on my neck.

She speaks Latin, whispering a single word into my ear.

"*Cruciatus.*"

And one by one, the vampires fall. The pain, all-encompassing and utterly excruciating, is everywhere. It is all I feel, all I smell, all I taste. It consumes my senses, my mind, my body.

I am on the ground, but I don't remember falling. I clutch my head, desperate to ease the throbbing within. My brain feels like it's on fire, like it's on the brink of exploding. Or maybe it already has. Maybe I am slowly bleeding to death, only to be healed by my magic just to succumb to this torment again. Over and over.

This. Is. Hell.

The last thing I see are the vampires. They too are on the ground, hunched over in anguish just as I am. Blood seeps from their eyes, from their ears. Screaming, they cower in pools of it.

My own blood streams down my face, and I choke on it as it erupts from my mouth. It cascades over my eyes, blinding me.

She hums as she leaves, amulet in hand, and as the darkness takes me, I have one final thought.

Both my sire and my amulet are now his.

ACKNOWLEDGMENTS

I am grateful for having so many inspiring people in my life who have worked tirelessly to support my writing career.

To my family and my readers—I couldn't do this without you. Seriously. You keep me sane and confident when things quickly go amuck, and your love for the worlds I create and encouragement to continue writing new ones never go unnoticed. I cherish you all more than I could ever explain.

To my publisher—I am both grateful and honored to be part of this publishing family. Thank you for your endless support.

ABOUT DANIELLE ROSE

Dubbed a "triple threat" by readers, Danielle Rose dabbles in many genres, including urban fantasy, suspense, and romance. The *USA Today* bestselling author holds a master of fine arts in creative writing from the University of Southern Maine.

Danielle is a self-professed sufferer of 'philes and an Oxford comma enthusiast. She prefers solitude to crowds, animals to people, four seasons to hellfire, nature to cities, and traveling as often as she breathes.

Visit her at DRoseAuthor.com

CONTINUE READING
THE DARKHAVEN SAGA

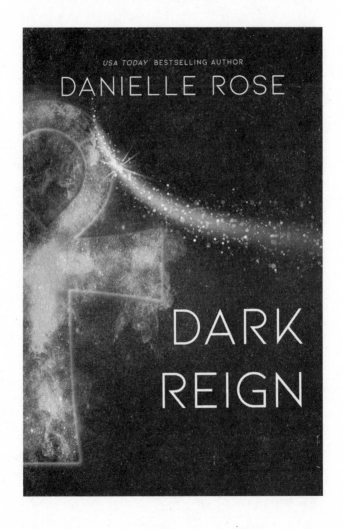